Laurie is only nineteen, and he has no intention of growing up anytime soon. His family still treats him like a child, and as long as that means he can continue having no responsibilities, he has no plans to change.

Alexis has everything planned. He's studying in college, working as a babysitter, and enjoying himself while keeping an eye on his goals.

Neither of them expected their life to change, but it does.

When Laurie finds out he has a daughter, he's tempted to run away and never look back. He would have, if her mother hadn't dumped the baby into his arms for the day and left. Meeting his mate while at the grocery store to buy diapers makes an already terrifying situation even scarier, but Laurie knows he doesn't have a choice.

He has to grow up — for Melissa, for Alexis, but also for himself.

Hopefully, Alexis will give him time to do that, because now that he's met him, Laurie can't imagine losing him.

Baby Steps
Copyright © 2021 Catherine Lievens
ISBN: 978-1-4874-3221-8
Cover art by Angela Waters

Published by eXtasy Books Inc or
Devine Destinies, an imprint of eXtasy Books Inc

Look for us online at:
www.eXtasybooks.com or www.devinedestinies.com

Baby Steps
Seven Brothers 4

By

Catherine Lievens

CHAPTER ONE

God, you're a dick. It's over.

Laurie stared at the text for a moment before dismissing it. He'd expected this to happen anyway. It always did after a while. Instead of answering his now ex-girlfriend, he opened the string of texts between him and Gilbert, his best friend. *Natalie just broke up with me.*

He leaned against the counter and quickly looked around the coffee shop. No one was waiting for coffee, and the few customers were busy. That meant he didn't have much to do right now, but his boss would still have his ass if he found him texting on the job. What was he supposed to do, though? Stand around waiting for someone to want coffee?

That didn't take long, Gilbert answered. *How long were you with her? A week?*

Laurie frowned. *Two, I think.*

A record. What happened?

Laurie hesitated. *I'm not sure.*

He could almost hear his best friend sigh. *Of course you aren't. I don't know why I asked. Where are you? Do you need me to come over?*

Laurie wanted to say yes, but Roger really would kill him if he did. *I'm at work, but I'm off in a few hours. Will you pick me up?*

Always. Didn't your boss say something about you not texting while you were working?

He's not here.

That doesn't mean he doesn't know you're texting. Gosh, Laurie.

1

You need to start acting like an adult.

Laurie scowled. *Why? I'm nineteen.*

Exactly. That means you are an adult, even though you don't seem to believe that.

I don't see why I should act like an adult when people don't view me as one. I can't even get a beer at the bar.

I see you don't want to talk, so I'll see you later.

Laurie stared at the screen for a few moments longer, hoping Gilbert would text something else. He was bored, and he wanted his best friend to distract him. Gilbert was gone, though, so Laurie sighed and put his phone away. When he looked up, he found his boss standing in the door that led to the break room, his arms crossed over his chest, glaring.

Laurie beamed at him, then grabbed the nearest towel and started scrubbing the counter. He saw Roger's shoulders slump, and the man moved closer.

"I don't know what I should do with you," Roger said.

Laurie was still grinning. "Give me a raise?"

"What for? You do half to work the other employees do. I should fire you."

"But you won't." Laurie batted his lashes. He usually dated girls, but he wasn't against using his charms to get himself out of being fired. Besides, his boss was kind of hot. Not Laurie's type, but he was good eye candy.

"Your mother would kill me," Roger said.

Usually, Laurie disliked living in a small town where everyone knew everyone, but he couldn't deny that sometimes it came in handy. Roger and Laurie's mother had gone to school together, and they were best friends. He would never do anything to hurt her, which included firing her youngest son. Roger didn't know that if Laurie's mother found out how he behaved, she would kick his ass herself, and Laurie wasn't about to tell him. He wasn't a complete idiot, whatever people usually thought.

"Can you at least *act* as if you're working?" Roger asked.

He rubbed the back of his neck, and his arm muscles bulged. Laurie eyed them, wondering how it would feel to be held down in bed.

He shook his head, not wanting to go down that road. "I am." He raised his towel. "See?"

"Go clean the tables."

Laurie beamed and walked around the counter. He'd won, just like always. It was starting to get boring, but he didn't know what else to do.

He supposed he could look into college, but he wasn't one for books and studying. That was one of the reasons people thought he was an idiot. The other was that he was the youngest of seven brothers, so everyone tended to look at him like a child anyway, even though he wasn't anymore. Tell that to his brothers and his parents, though.

Laurie had stopped trying to convince them he was worthy. He'd decided just to do what he wanted in life, which, right now, was working at the shop. It would change eventually, although he didn't know what he would do when it did. He liked his job, even though he didn't do much — or maybe because of that.

That didn't mean he could see himself doing this for the rest of his life. He was nineteen, and this was a nice first job, but unless Laurie was planning on buying the shop, he had bigger plans for himself. What those plans were, he had no idea, but he would figure it out sooner or later. In the meantime, he promised himself he would have fun, and he had every intention of keeping that promise.

He softly snorted, making a girl sitting two tables down look at him. He grinned, and she smiled back. He didn't want to think about how he never kept promises, even the ones he made to himself. His mother already bothered him enough about it, and while he couldn't avoid her lectures, he *could* avoid lecturing himself, especially at work.

He moved toward the girl. "Hi there. Can I get you any-thing else?" he said, tilting his chin toward her coffee.

"I don't know. Do you think you can sit with me if I get another coffee?"

"Of course."

"Won't your boss get angry?"

"He's a big teddy bear, so don't worry about that. What did you get again? I'll grab you a second one and something for me."

If Laurie was lucky, he would end the day with a girlfriend, and it wouldn't be Natalie.

Roger looked desperate while Laurie walked around the counter to make two coffees, but thankfully, he didn't say an-ything. Laurie knew he was maybe pushing too much and that he would have to change something, but he wasn't ready for that yet.

Everyone looked at him and saw a child. If that was what they wanted, it was what he was going to give them.

By the time the girl—Sarah—left the coffee shop, Laurie had her number saved in his phone. They weren't dating yet, but that was only because she wasn't sure when she would have the time to go out with him. She was in college, and it was a lot of work, which was one of the reasons Laurie had no intention of ever going. He already had enough brainiacs in his family. He didn't need to add to it.

"I need you in the stockroom," Roger said when Laurie was done cleaning the table.

"Why? I'd rather work here."

"I know, which is why I'm sending you to the back. And if you were wondering, I'm your boss, and I'm the one who gives orders here. Unless you're planning on buying the shop from me, you're supposed to obey."

Laurie smiled. "I'm aware you're the boss." He gave Roger an impressed once over, smiling even wider when Roger's cheeks flushed.

"Stop trying to flirt with me. I know you're not into me, and nothing you do or say will change that," Roger snapped. He sucked in a breath. "Just go."

Laurie didn't mind. At least in the stockroom, he could sit down and not look like he was supposed to be busy.

By the time Laurie's workday was over, he'd texted back and forth with Sarah, and he was pretty sure they would have their first date this week, or maybe the next. It was a bit too far in the future for him, but it wasn't like he couldn't find someone else if he wanted to. As long as they were nothing like Natalie, he didn't really care who he dated.

His phone rang just as he stepped out of the shop. He waved at Gilbert, who was sitting in his car waiting for him, and rushed toward him as he answered. "Yes?" He hoped it was Sarah, but he should have checked first.

"Finally. I was sure you were dead in a ditch somewhere," his mother drawled.

Laurie huffed as he slid into the car. "You're not funny, Mom. What do you want?"

"Just to know if you're coming over for dinner."

"I don't know. I just got off work, and I need to go home. I don't like smelling of coffee for the rest of the evening."

"You should still have time to come over for dinner, though. I'll be waiting for you."

"I didn't say I was coming!" It was too late. She'd already hung up, and he glared at his phone until the screen turned black.

"We should go," Gilbert said.

"I thought you were on my side."

"I am. I also love your mom, though."

"I have no idea why," Laurie grumbled. But he did. Gilbert had lost his mom when he was a teenager, and he'd pretty much lived with Laurie and his family after that. "Fine,"

Laurie added. "We can go." He suspected he would regret this, but Gilbert was one of the few people he truly cared about, and he wanted his best friend to be happy. If having dinner with his family made that happen, then Laurie would suffer through it.

Alexis cooed at his brother and wiggled his fingertips for Mark to grab. Mark laughed, as if that was the best thing in the world, and Alexis suspected that for him, it was. After all, Mark was only two.

"What do you want to do now?" Alexis asked.

"Eat!" Mark yelled.

Alexis smiled. "How did I know that would be your answer?" He tickled Mark's stomach. "All right. Let me see what we have in the fridge." He already knew his mother would have something healthy for the baby. She always made sure she did, especially when Alexis babysat for her.

Mark was settled in his highchair with some cut-up cherry tomatoes and a bit of cheese when the front door banged open. Alexis didn't have to ask to know who had arrived, and he waited for the tornado that was his sister to walk into the kitchen.

When she did, she made a beeline for Mark, who grinned at her with his mouth full. That gave Celine pause, but she still kissed the top of Mark's head before turning to Alexis. "That's disgusting," she commented as she leaned over to kiss Alexis's cheek.

Alexis chuckled. "What, you didn't want to know what he was eating?"

"I would rather have looked at his plate. What are you doing here?"

"What does it look like I'm doing? Babysitting."

She shook her head and sat down. Mark was focused on

his food again, and he would barely look at them for the next ten to fifteen minutes. "I don't get it."

"Which is why Mom asks me to babysit instead of you." That and the fact that Alexis needed the money for college and that he was studying education. He supposed he was a perfect babysitter, as far as his mother was concerned.

"Don't you get enough of this at college?"

"I don't get enough of Mark, no." Alexis smiled softly. "I love taking care of him."

When their mother had told them that she was having a baby a few years ago, it had been a surprise. Celine was already sixteen, while Alexis was twenty-one. Neither of them had thought their parents would have another child, yet here they were.

It hadn't been easy for Celine to get used to it. Alexis was already out of the house by the time Mark was born, but she hadn't been, and she'd had to learn to deal with diaper changes and nighttime feedings. Alexis knew how hard it could be and that Celine was happier now that she'd left the house to move in with a friend.

Celine was still looking at him, and Alexis waited for her to ask what was on her mind. "You really don't care?" she finally said.

"About the babysitting?"

"Yeah. I did it when I still lived here, and I couldn't wait for it to end."

"It doesn't bother me. I wouldn't be studying education if it did."

"I thought you were going to teach older kids."

"I don't know." It was tempting, but there was something sweet about babies and toddlers. Their life was so much easier, and Alexis didn't want to deal with moody teenagers. He supposed that a moody toddler could be scarier, though.

"Well, better you than me," Celine added.

"Tell me about you," Alexis said, changing the topic of their conversation. They talked about it every time they saw each other and Mark was there, and it was getting boring. Celine already knew he loved babysitting, even though she clearly didn't believe him.

"Nothing much to say. I'm going out with Michelle tonight. What about you? Will you still be babysitting?"

Alexis shook his head. "Mom should be back in an hour or two."

Celine bounced on her chair. "Does that mean you're going out?"

"I don't know. I have to study."

She huffed. "You're always studying or babysitting. You need to go out more, Alexis. You're only twenty-four. You're not dead yet."

Alexis glared. "I'm very much aware of that." He leaned forward and caught Mark's sippy cup before he could launch it onto the floor. He put it back onto the tray and gently glared at him, making Mark laugh.

When Alexis sat back down, Celine was staring at him. It made him self-conscious, and he looked away. "I know I'm not dead," he told his sister.

"Then stop acting like it. People are always surprised when I tell them about you, because from the way I describe you, it sounds like you're eighty."

"Don't describe me that way, then."

"I'm just telling the truth. I'm not saying you have to go out until two in the morning and get drunk every opportunity you have, but live a little. When are you going to do it? Once you're done with college and have a job? After you're married and have your own kids?"

"Who said anything about having kids?" Even though it was something Alexis wanted in the future, the thought of doing it anytime soon was terrifying. He already had more than enough on his plate.

Celine rolled her eyes. "Don't look so scared. I didn't say you had to have them now. It's just something to think about. You have a lot of responsibilities already, and it's only going to get worse as you get older."

She wasn't wrong. Alexis already felt overwhelmed, and he was only dealing with college, babysitting Mark, and his job. What would it be like to add his own family to that? "I'll call Colton and see if he wants to go out tonight."

Celine beamed. "That's what I'm talking about. I don't expect you to do anything over the top or stupid like other people your age are doing, but stepping away from the books and the babysitting for an evening won't hurt. If anything, it'll help you relax, and you sorely need that."

"I already said I'd call Colton. There's no need to continue pushing."

She grinned. "I wouldn't be your little sister if I wasn't pushing."

At that moment, Mark threw a quarter of a cherry tomato in Celine's face. It hit her forehead, making both Mark and Alexis laugh. Celine glared at Alexis, but he could see she was trying to suppress a smile.

"That's not funny," she said.

"Mark and I beg to disagree. It was hilarious." He turned toward Mark and held his hand up. "That wasn't nice, buddy," he told him. No matter how much he enjoyed watching his sister get smacked by a cherry tomato, Mark needed to learn he couldn't throw food. "What did I tell you about throwing things?"

Mark pouted, but he didn't answer. He was a master of not answering questions he didn't like, and Alexis knew he wouldn't get anything out of him, so he let it go.

He handed a napkin to Celine. "Use this."

"I don't understand why you want to make this your life,

but better you than me, I guess."

"It's not that bad." At least Alexis knew how to deal with Mark. He had a harder time when it came to adults.

He didn't understand games and had no patience for one-night stands. He didn't get why people were so interested in them. What was so good about having sex with a person and never seeing them again? Wouldn't it be better to see that person again and again and fall in love? That was one of the reasons he didn't go out much, although mainly it was because he was so busy. He supposed that tonight, though, he and Colton would get a beer somewhere. He might be grumpy about it, but he was also looking forward to it. It had been too long since he and Colton had spent time together, and he missed his best friend.

Tomorrow, Alexis would be back in his books and in the house that he'd grown up in, babysitting his baby brother.

Laurie was nervous, just like every time he had to meet his family. It wouldn't be so bad if he only had to deal with his parents, but at least a few of his brothers were bound to be there, too, and he could have done without dealing with them. Hugh, Curtis, and Sean were easier because they were so focused on their mates that they barely noticed anything else. On the other hand, Jack and Andy wouldn't hesitate to tease Laurie about anything they could think about. Laurie supposed he should feel lucky that Richie probably wouldn't be home, but instead, he was worried. It wasn't like him, but it had been too long since Richie had spent any time with the family, and it made Laurie's skin prickle with unease. He couldn't help wondering if something had happened to Richie, although he supposed their parents would know if that was the case.

"We don't have to go if you don't want to," Gilbert said

from the driver's seat.

Laurie resisted the urge to roll his eyes. "I know you want to."

"I don't understand why you don't. They're your family. They love you, and they want to spend time with you."

"Your father wants to spend time with you, too."

Gilbert grimaced. "I wouldn't be too sure about that."

"He's your father. Why wouldn't he?"

Gilbert looked at Laurie strangely. "You're serious, aren't you?"

Laurie frowned. "Why wouldn't I be?"

"Do you even bother listening when I talk?" There was a hint of anger in Gilbert's voice, and Laurie wondered what was going on.

He tried to think back, but nothing came to mind. "What's going on?"

Gilbert huffed. "Nothing. Don't worry about it."

"You know that saying that will make me wonder even more."

Instead of answering, Gilbert parked the car. Laurie hadn't realized they were already there, and he didn't want the conversation to be over. He wished Gilbert would tell him what was happening. They were best friends, and Laurie never hesitated to unburden himself when he needed to. Gilbert should do the same.

But Gilbert was already out of the car, and Laurie could only follow him. He wanted to push, but it was obvious Gilbert didn't want to talk about whatever was happening. He was hurrying away from Laurie, and even though Laurie tried to catch up to him, he already had the front door open when Laurie did.

The smell of cooking and the sound of loud voices hit Laurie at the same time. He took a step back, then breathed deeply and followed Gilbert inside.

To his surprise, Gilbert was still hovering in the hallway, looking around. "What?" Laurie asked. "You changed your mind?"

Gilbert shook his head. "Do you know who's going to be here?"

"What do you mean?"

"Your brothers. Do you know which of them are coming?"

"I have no idea, but I suppose Jack and Andy are. Why?"

"Just asking."

Laurie frowned. "You're looking forward to seeing them?"

That made Gilbert smile. "Why wouldn't I? They're great."

Laurie had to stomp down the hint of jealousy that threatened to bubble over. Gilbert had spent most of his teenage years in the house with Laurie. After his mother died, his father had been working a lot. Laurie's mother had adopted him unofficially, and even though he wasn't a Long brother, he might as well be. Laurie was his best friend, but he was friends with all of Laurie's brothers, except maybe Richie.

"Look who's here!" Andy yelled.

Laurie couldn't even bring himself to smile. He watched Andy and Jack barrel toward Gilbert as if Laurie barely existed.

"It's our favorite brother," Andy continued.

Jack bumped his shoulder against Andy's. "Don't say that. We wouldn't be able to flirt with him if he was our brother."

Andy beamed. "True that." He wrapped an arm around Gilbert's shoulders and squeezed. "We missed you. Where have you been?"

They guided Gilbert into the living room, and Laurie was left trailing behind. He only followed because he didn't want to spend the evening in the entrance, but he wished he could go back to Gilbert's car and ignore this family dinner. He hadn't wanted to come in the first place, and now he remembered exactly why.

"What's this?" Laurie's father asked as he walked into the living room, drying his hands. His eyes went wide when he saw Gilbert, and he turned to Laurie. "I didn't think you'd come. Your mother said you wouldn't."

Laurie smiled awkwardly and tried to ignore the trio still teasing each other. "We changed our mind."

Laurie's father smiled. "Good. You know we're always happy to see you and Gilbert."

"I know." And he indeed did. He just had to get over the jealousy over not having Gilbert to himself.

Gilbert was the only stable person in Laurie's life, apart from his family. Laurie had girlfriend after girlfriend, and they disappeared just as fast as they appeared. Gilbert was different, though, and Laurie had a hard time sharing him with anyone, especially his brothers. They all had their own lives and their own best friends. Why did they have to try to get their hands on Gilbert, too?

Laurie was aware that he was grumpy and that his family was starting to wonder why, but he didn't care. He stayed mostly silent during dinner, no matter how much his mother tried to coax him into a conversation. She kept asking questions he didn't want to answer anyway. He couldn't remember who he'd been with the last time he'd mentioned he had a girlfriend, and she was bound to say something about it if he got it wrong. He didn't want to talk to his mother about his love life anyway, and he decided that keeping his mouth shut would be better for everyone, but especially him.

By the time dinner was over, he almost ran out the door. Gilbert followed at a more sedate pace, still chatting with Andy and Jack. He only stopped once he was in the car, the door closed behind him. Andy and Jack were still on the porch, waving, and Gilbert waved back and chuckled.

"I love your brothers," he said with a sigh.

"Then why don't you become best friends with them?"

Laurie snapped.

Gilbert blinked, but thankfully, he managed to drive away. Laurie didn't think he could have stood watching his brothers simper over Gilbert any longer.

"What do you mean?" Gilbert asked.

"You're so cozy with them. Maybe you'd like having them as your best friends."

"You're an asshole," Gilbert snapped back.

His tone of voice was enough to give Laurie pause. "What are you talking about? I didn't say anything that's not true."

"The fact that you don't know is even worse and shows how selfish you are."

Laurie was shocked. He wanted to leave, but Gilbert was driving, and unless Laurie wanted to throw himself out the door, he wasn't going anywhere. "I'm not selfish."

Gilbert snorted. "You're the most selfish person I know, Laurie. You bitch about your family and your brothers, and you don't even realize how lucky you are to have them. Yes, I spent most of the evening with Jack and Andy. You know why? Because to me, they're like brothers, and I don't have brothers. They're the closest thing I can have to a family, and I don't want to give that up, not even because you're annoyed."

"I'm not annoyed. But I'm your best friend, not them."

"That's what I was talking about. You only see your own feelings. For you, it's only Laurie, Laurie, Laurie. You don't care how I feel. You don't care that I like coming here for dinner, spending time with your parents and your brothers. You don't care that it makes me feel like I still have a family."

"You have your father."

At those words, Gilbert looked even angrier. "You really don't listen to me when I talk, do you?"

"That's not true."

"What did I tell you about my father, then? Something

happened with him, and I told you about it. Can you tell me what it is?"

Laurie had no idea, and evidently it only took Gilbert a few seconds to realize that. Once he did, he turned his full attention back to the road and ignored Laurie until they got to Laurie's apartment. Even once there, he barely said goodbye.

"I'll see you soon?" Laurie asked.

Gilbert sighed, and his shoulders slumped. "I want to say I don't want to see you until you grow up a bit, but I doubt that's going to happen anytime soon, so yes. I guess I'll see you soon."

For some reason, that didn't make Laurie feel any better.

Alexis smiled and relaxed. He hadn't believed going out with Colton would help even after Celine had insisted, but she'd been right. He would never admit that to her face, but he'd needed some time off work and college to focus on his friends.

"I'd given up hope that you'd want to come out with us," Colton said, knocking their shoulders together.

Alexis glared at him, but they both knew there was no heat in it. "You think you're funny, don't you?"

"I *know* I'm funny," Colton answered. He leaned the other way toward his girlfriend, Serena. "Aren't I?"

"You're hilarious," she deadpanned, making Alexis laugh and Colton scowl at her.

"I knew you weren't that much under his charm," Alexis told her.

"I might be, but I'm not blind, nor an idiot. He's the only one who thinks he's funny. I'm happy to have support when it comes to that. I thought you'd never stop babysitting to come out with us."

Alexis had to work hard to keep his smile on his face. "You know how it is."

Serena shrugged. "Not really. I don't understand why a guy would want to do that. You couldn't pay me enough to spend time with people under twenty."

"Can you stop that?" Colton snapped.

Serena's smile faltered. "What? I'm just telling him what I think. Who wants to play babysitter for the rest of their life? That's what you're studying, isn't it?" she asked Alexis.

Alexis winced. It wasn't the first time people thought he was studying to be a glorified babysitter. He wished he could slap every single person who ever said that, but he would be slapping pretty much everyone. It wasn't worth the effort. "That's not what I would call it, but I *am* studying education."

"See?" Serena asked, turning back to Colton. "He wants to take care of kids."

"He wants to be a *teacher*. That's a great thing, and I don't like the way you're talking about it."

Alexis reached out and gently touched Colton's forearm. "Let it go," he murmured.

Colton twisted on his stool to face Alexis, effectively dismissing Serena without adding a word. Alexis heard her huff in annoyance, and he was grateful he wouldn't have to deal with her later. Colton, on the other hand, would have his hands full. "You shouldn't have done that," he told his best friend.

"Done what?"

"You antagonized your girlfriend. That's not a nice thing to do."

"What's not a nice thing to do is telling you that you're little more than a glorified babysitter. She knows that's not the case. I already talked to her about this, and I can't believe she went there. I'm sorry."

Alexis shook his head. He was grateful for Colton's support, and it made him love the guy even more, but he didn't need it. He also didn't need Colton to fight with his girlfriend over him. "Don't apologize. You didn't do anything, and neither did Serena. I'm used to it."

"You shouldn't be. It's not right."

"But it's my battle to fight, not yours."

Colton shook his head. "It is in this case. I don't want to be with someone who belittles you that way."

"Does that mean you don't want to be with me?" Serena snapped.

Alexis sighed. He'd tried, but obviously, he'd failed, and he suspected Colton and Serena were going to spend some time bickering over him. He wanted nothing to do with it, so he slid off the stool and headed toward the other side of the bar. Hopefully, putting some distance between them would help Colton and Serena.

He hadn't wanted them to fight, but he was grateful for Colton's support. It had taken him some time to accept what he wanted to do with his life. He didn't think it was stupid. There were plenty of male teachers in the country, after all. Why couldn't he be one? But a lot of people thought it was a job for women, especially when it came to younger kids, and while Alexis didn't care, he could do without the snickering and insinuations. He supposed he should get used to it. He couldn't imagine that dealing with parents was any easier than dealing with children. If anything, it was probably more challenging.

He waved at the bartender, who nodded at him. Alexis leaned against the counter and looked around the bar, grimacing at the sight of Colton and Serena still hissing at each other. Then his gaze drifted, and it paused on Laurie Long.

It wasn't the first time Alexis had seen him around. He and Laurie had never talked, but Celine knew him, which meant Alexis did, too. His sister and Laurie were the same age, and Alexis knew everything there was to know about the guy through his sister. When she was younger especially, she'd decided that since he was gay, he wouldn't mind hearing about her crushes and the boys she was friends with. She'd spent many hours chattering on about guys, Laurie in particular. From what Alexis knew, it was better if Celine stayed away from the guy, and he was relieved she had.

Laurie was flitting around the room, just like always. It wasn't the first time Alexis had noticed him, but he'd never wanted to talk to him, and he still didn't. Still, he couldn't deny the guy was cute, and watching him was amusing. As it was, Laurie had managed to flirt his way to getting a beer, even though he was underage. Alexis was pretty sure that if the bartender noticed, he would kick Laurie's ass out, but the guy was so busy he probably hadn't. As it was, Laurie was making sure the woman who had bought it for him hid him from sight, which made Alexis smile.

"You wanted something?" the bartender asked.

Alexis turned to face him. "A beer."

The guy had already served him earlier, so he knew Alexis was twenty-four, since he'd carded him. Thankfully, he didn't ask for Alexis's ID again, and once Alexis had his beer, he took a sip and relaxed. Every so often, he peeked toward Colton and Serena, but they'd disappeared somewhere. He was pretty sure they were outside, either still fighting or fucking against the wall. He wouldn't be surprised by either.

Since they weren't there anymore, Alexis found himself looking for Laurie again. He didn't have anything better to do, and he should waste some time until Colton returned.

Laurie's beer was empty, and he was talking with a different woman. There was no sign of the one who'd bought him the beer, and Alexis wondered if Laurie had already dismissed her.

As much as Alexis didn't understand why people would want a one-night stand, he knew Laurie was a master at it. Every time Alexis had seen him at the bar, he'd been with a different girl. It made Alexis wonder if Laurie even remembered their names. Not that he cared. He had no intention of becoming Laurie's friend, and the only reason he was thinking about him was that he was alone right now.

He took another sip of beer and gently snorted to himself. Okay, so maybe he was watching Laurie because Laurie was worth watching. Alexis had only ever seen him with girls, but that didn't mean Laurie wasn't gorgeous. He was slightly shorter than Alexis, from what Alexis could tell, and his skin looked like he spent a lot of time in the sun. His hair was brown and slightly too long, with highlights that looked too good to come from a bottle. His body was trim and thin, and his ass was perfectly round.

Alexis could too easily imagine what a handful of it would feel like, so he turned back toward the bar. It was one thing to watch Laurie to distract himself, but it was another to lust over him, especially since they didn't know each other and probably never would. There was no reason for Alexis to talk to Laurie or for Laurie to be interested in Alexis.

Alexis didn't have enough boobs for Laurie to even look at him.

"Here you are," Colton said.

Alexis looked him up and down, trying to understand what had happened with Serena. Colton's hair was all over the place, but his lips weren't red the way they usually were when he and Serena made out. His clothes were neat, so it didn't look like he and Serena had made peace in the alley outside the bar.

"What happened?"

Colton shook his head and sat down on an empty stool next to Alexis. "Nothing. Serena went home, though."

Alexis sighed. "You know I don't want the two of you to fight over me."

"I don't care what you want, not when it comes to this. If

she can't respect you, I don't want to be with her."

"Please tell me you didn't break up with her over this."

"Not yet."

But it was implied that eventually, he might. Alexis didn't know how to feel about it, but he supposed it wasn't any of his business. This was Colton's life, not his, and even though he didn't want Colton to do that, he didn't have a say in it, especially not when he was grateful. Colton was his best friend and had stood up for Alexis the way Alexis would stand up for him if he needed to.

CHAPTER TWO

L aurie's apartment wasn't great. He would be the first one to admit it if anyone but his family asked. He always said that he was more than happy to live here when it came to them, and it wasn't a lie. The apartment might be crappy, but it came with no family, no parents, and no brothers, which made it the perfect place for him to live.

What also made it the perfect place was that no one told him what to do, which was why he was stretched out on his couch on a Friday morning, wearing only sweatpants and playing with his phone. He didn't have to go to work today, and he had every intention of spending the day doing nothing.

That was, he had every intention of doing nothing until someone knocked on the door.

Laurie stared at it. He had no idea who it could be. His mother refused to come over because she hated the place, and while his brothers didn't care much, they also didn't have a reason to visit him. Could it be Gilbert? They hadn't separated on the best of terms last night, but Gilbert had said they would see each other soon. He wasn't one to hold a grudge, thankfully, even though Laurie still couldn't remember what Gilbert had told him about his father.

There was a second knock, and Laurie knew he would have to get up and open. Gilbert had a key, so he doubted that was who it was, which didn't bode well. Whoever was there really wanted to talk to him, and he quickly tried to remember if he owed anyone money. He always paid his bills on time since the first time he'd forgotten and had to run to his parents for help. That had been humiliating, and he never wanted it to happen again. He could stand on his own two feet — mostly — and he wanted his family to know that even though they probably didn't care much.

At the third knock, Laurie hauled himself up. "I'm coming!"

He looked around. The apartment was a bit of a mess, but he didn't have time to clean up. Besides, he doubted that whoever was there would come in. He strode to the door and flung it open, ready to tell whoever it was to fuck off, but he froze.

"Candace?"

She stood in the doorway holding a baby, of all things. Candace was one of Laurie's ex-girlfriends, and he tried to remember the last time he'd seen her, but he couldn't. It had been at least a year, if not more. She was still as pretty, all blonde hair and blue eyes. She also looked annoyed, a look she'd sported many times when they'd been together. Their relationship had been one of the longest Laurie had, which meant it had lasted about a month.

He had no idea what to think of the baby, though.

"I thought you weren't going to answer," Candace grumbled.

"Sorry. It's my day off, and I wasn't expecting anyone."

Candace looked him up and down.

Laurie felt she was examining him and judging him, and the thought made him shuffle his feet.

"That much is obvious." She peeked around Laurie into the apartment and grimaced. "Not great, but I suppose it's going to have to do."

"What are you talking about? And what are you doing here?" Laurie wanted to ask about the baby she was holding, but he was kind of scared. He'd never had to deal with a baby, and he never wanted to.

Candace looked at him straight in the eyes. "This is Melissa. She's your daughter."

Laurie blinked. "My what?"

"You heard me." Candace shifted, and Laurie found himself with an armful of baby.

He didn't want to take her, but the only other option was to let her go, and even though he was an asshole, he didn't want to hurt the baby. "I don't have children," he said stupidly.

Candace arched a delicate brow. "I beg to differ. I carried her for nine months, and I know she's yours. You were the only boyfriend I had at the time."

Melissa was all wiggly and trying to grab Laurie's nose for some reason, and he angled his face the other way. "This isn't possible. We used condoms."

"Yeah, well, sometimes, they don't work. She's proof of that." Candace looked at her watch. "Anyway, I have to go. I'll be back this afternoon." She unhooked a bag from her shoulder and left it on the floor. "There's food for her in here, but you're going to have to buy her diapers. There are only a few left. Sorry about that, but I didn't have time to go to the grocery store."

What the fuck was going on? "You can't leave her here." Panic was settling in Laurie's chest, and he'd never dealt well with that.

"Why not? She's your daughter, which means she's your responsibility."

"We have to talk about it. And really, do I look like I can take care of a baby?"

Candace's expression softened for a moment. Melissa stuffed her fist into her mouth, and Laurie looked in horror as she started drooling.

"I know you have no idea what to do with her. I didn't,

either, when I had her. You better get used to it. I'm not doing this on my own."

"You've already done this on your own! You were pregnant, and you didn't tell me. What changed? Why are you here?" Laurie didn't even know how old Melissa was, although it couldn't be more than a few months.

Candace shook her head. "I don't have time to talk now. I promise I'll be back tonight. Remember to go to the grocery store. Melissa isn't a hard baby to deal with, so you shouldn't have too many problems. I left you a note in the diaper bag, so make sure to read it. That way, you'll know everything you need to know."

Laurie opened his mouth to answer, but at that moment, Melissa opened her mouth, slipped her fist out of it, and started wailing.

Laurie winced. He'd never heard anything more horrible than that sounded. He tried to shush her, and when he turned around to tell Candace that he couldn't take care of a baby, she was already next to the elevator, barely looking back. She slipped through the doors before he could stop her, and they closed behind her, leaving him alone with Melissa.

She was still crying.

Laurie patted her back and moved her up and down, looking around for help. No one was there, though. The only person he could think of calling right now was his mother, but she would kill him if she found out he had a daughter.

Laurie's knees went weak. He had a *daughter*. He was a *father*. How the fuck had that happened? He'd always been so careful, because he never wanted something like this to happen. He was only nineteen, for fuck's sake. He didn't know anything, and he especially didn't know how to deal with a baby. He'd never intended to have a child, yet here he was, with a crying Melissa in the middle of the hallway.

He hooked his foot around the bag and dragged it inside

before stepping into his apartment and closing the door. The last thing he needed was for one of his neighbors to come out to check what was happening. Once the door was closed behind him, he looked down at Melissa, trying to figure out what to do. Babies couldn't be that complicated to deal with, could they? Candace had said that Melissa was an easy baby, yet to Laurie, it didn't look like it.

"Okay, okay," he murmured, still moving Melissa up and down and stroking her back. "Are you hungry?" He could probably deal with making her a bottle of milk, but what if that wasn't the problem?

What if he had to change her diaper?

The thought almost made him run in horror, but even though he had no idea what he was doing, he couldn't abandon Melissa. For now, she was his responsibility. He would make sure to tell Candace what he thought of her dumping Melissa into his arms and running away, though. He couldn't do this. He couldn't deal with a baby, and he couldn't be a father.

In the meantime, it looked like he was going to have to learn to change a diaper, and he prayed it wasn't as hard as he thought it was.

Alexis grabbed some bread and dropped it into his cart, then checked his list. He enjoyed this moment of respite, and he supposed people would think him weird to know he liked grocery shopping. There was something soothing about it, at least to him. For half an hour, he could leave everything else behind and not think about college, his job, or even babysitting Mark. Right now, he was alone, and his only responsibility was to remember to get laundry soap.

He needed a distraction anyway. Colton had called him this morning, and he'd admitted that he and Serena had been fighting over what had happened last night. Alexis hadn't wanted that to happen, but Colton had insisted he didn't care. If Serena couldn't take what Alexis did for a living seriously, she wasn't the kind of woman Colton wanted to be with. Alexis wasn't sure he was important enough to warrant that kind of behavior, but he couldn't exactly tell his best friend who to date—or not to date. He liked Serena, but he could admit he didn't enjoy how she looked down at him for enjoying working with children. He would be sad for Colton if they broke up, but knowing Colton, it wouldn't take him long to have someone else in his life. Hopefully, the next person would be more accepting of Alexis's work.

Alexis rounded the corner into a different aisle. He could hear a baby crying somewhere in the store, and his fingers itched to find it and soothe it. He wasn't on the job right now, though, and he didn't want to antagonize what might be a new mother. From the sound of it, the baby was fairly young, and it could take some time to get used to life with a little one and how to deal with them.

Alexis tried to focus on his grocery shopping, but it was hard to ignore the wailing. It was becoming louder and louder with every second that passed, and when he finally turned into the aisle where the diapers were located, he found the source of the noise.

Laurie Long was standing in the middle of the aisle, looking terrified as he checked diapers. He was holding a baby with one arm, and he was moving from side to side and trying to soothe her while he picked up diapers with his other, looking at them then putting them back. He stopped every so often to look at the baby, but nothing he was doing helped, and Alexis wasn't surprised.

It was obvious Laurie had no idea what to do with the baby.

Alexis hesitated. This wasn't his business, and he should

stay far away from Laurie. He wasn't the new mother Alexis had expected to find, but he clearly wasn't used to dealing with babies, and he might need some help. Besides, Alexis would be doing this for the baby more than for Laurie. The little one was still crying, and while Alexis didn't know what they needed, he knew how to deal with this kind of situation.

Alexis sighed and left his cart on one side of the aisle. "What are you doing?" he asked Laurie.

Laurie looked at him with wide eyes. "What?"

Alexis rolled his eyes and reached for the baby. "Come on. I can help."

He was surprised to see Laurie's hold on the baby tightening, as if he didn't trust Alexis. Maybe he wasn't that bad at taking care of the baby after all. He wasn't handing the baby to a stranger, which was a good first step, but the baby was still crying.

Alexis cleared his throat. It was hard to make himself heard above the wailing, but he had to try. "My name is Alexis. I think you know my sister, Celine."

Laurie looked more confused than ever. "I do."

"Well, you probably don't know that I'm a great babysitter and that I'm studying to be a teacher. I don't mean to offend you, but it's clear you don't know what to do with this baby, and I'd like to help."

Laurie looked like he couldn't dump the baby into Alexis's arms fast enough now that he knew who Alexis was. "Please. She started crying, and I don't know how to make her stop. I managed back at the apartment by changing her diaper, but it's clean now, and I don't know what to do."

So the baby was a girl. It was good to know. Alexis moved closer to get a good hold on the baby before Laurie let her go, and that took him close enough to Laurie to smell him.

The smell of baby was overpowering, but it couldn't hide the scent coming from Laurie.

The scent of *mate.*

Alexis almost backed away, but just then, Laurie deposited the baby into his arms. He was the one who suddenly backed up, his eyes even wider than before as he stared at Alexis.

Alexis groaned. This wasn't what he'd expected when he'd entered the grocery store, but before he could think about Laurie and his own feelings about them being mates, he had to focus on the baby.

He settled her into his arms more securely and gently rubbed her back. "What's her name?"

"Melissa."

Laurie was still staring, and Alexis could see he was freaking out. He wasn't Alexis's priority right now, though, so Alexis dismissed him and turned his attention to Melissa. "What's going on with you?" he murmured. "When did she last eat?" he asked Laurie.

"I don't know. Her mother dumped her on me this morning, and she told me I had to go to the grocery store to buy her diapers." He fumbled with something in his pocket. "Here. She left me this note in the diaper bag."

Alexis took the note and quickly went over it. Whoever Melissa's mother was, she'd been precise. She'd written when Melissa was supposed to eat, and sure enough, it was almost time.

Alexis handed the note back to Laurie. "You have the diaper bag?"

Laurie nodded and then handed it to Alexis. He hesitated, probably realizing that Alexis was still holding Melissa, but Alexis was used to this, too. He'd juggled babies and diaper bags more often than he could count, so he quickly found the bottle Melissa needed to drink. It only took him a few moments to unwrap the bottle containing hot water and add the formula. He mixed everything, tried the temperature on the inside of his wrist, then put Melissa in the correct position and popped the bottle into her mouth.

She started sucking right away. Alexis's ears still rang from the crying, but at least now, Melissa was calming down.

"She was hungry," Laurie said as he couldn't quite believe it.

"It happens fairly often when they're this young."

"I should have known. Gosh, I don't know what to do with her. What was Candace thinking?"

Laurie agreed that Melissa's mother hadn't been thinking. Even if Laurie was the father—and Alexis was pretty sure he was because he could see hints of him in Melissa—you couldn't just dump a baby with someone who didn't know what to do with one.

There was also the fact that he and Laurie were mates. Both of them were ignoring it, but they wouldn't be able to forever, even though it was tempting, especially with the baby between them.

"So Melissa is your daughter?" he asked instead of focusing on the mate thing.

Laurie raked a hand through his hair. Usually, when Alexis saw him, it was always perfectly styled. Today, it was a fluffy mess, and it made Laurie look more human and approachable, which was the last thing Alexis needed. He'd always found Laurie attractive, but right now, with his hair all over the place and the baby, he was everything Alexis had ever dreamed of.

And of course, there was the fact that they were mates.

Laurie didn't know what to do. What the fuck had happened to his day? He was supposed to spend it on his couch, not doing anything except maybe texting Gilbert or Sarah, the girl he'd met at the coffee shop yesterday. Instead, here he was, with a baby and his mate.

What would happen next?

He'd been clamping down on the panic bubbling in his chest ever since Candace had left Melissa with him, but it was getting harder now that he'd met Alexis. He wanted to run away and never look back. He didn't want the responsibilities of having a baby or a mate, and he had no idea how to deal with them. Anyone who knew him was aware that he didn't do well with responsibilities. It was a miracle he had his own apartment and a job, and he wasn't stupid enough not to realize that he wouldn't even have that if his mother wasn't friends with Roger.

How the fuck was he supposed to be a father and a mate?

He needed to focus on one problem at a time, and since there was nothing he could do about Melissa, he could ignore the fact that Alexis was his mate. Melissa needed him. Alexis didn't.

Laurie didn't even really know who Alexis was, for fuck's sake. He vaguely remembered Celine, mostly because when he'd asked her out, she'd refused. It didn't happen often, and he'd been stunned. He didn't think he'd ever known she had a brother, and even though Alexis was coming in handy right now, Laurie wanted to grab Melissa and run away with her.

He couldn't deal with a mate, not right now, and possibly not ever. He'd never wanted to meet his mate, and he'd never expected it to be a man. He was pan, but he usually dated girls, and he'd thought that if he ever met his mate, it would be a girl.

Alexis clearly wasn't.

He was taller than Laurie, with brown curls and blue eyes, and seeing him with the baby in his arms made Laurie want to climb him like a tree. He might even have done so if Alexis hadn't been his mate and if he hadn't been holding Laurie's daughter. Laurie was still trying to wrap his mind around that, let alone finding out he had a mate.

At least Melissa had stopped crying.

"Well, now that I know she needed to be fed, I can continue on my own," he said, reaching for Melissa.

Alexis took a step back. "You said you needed to buy diapers."

Laurie glared at him. He couldn't very well tear Melissa out of Alexis's arms, no matter how much he wanted to. "I do." He supposed that as long as they weren't talking about the fact that they were mates, he could go along with this. As soon as Alexis mentioned anything about that, though, he was out of here.

"You know what size she wears?"

Laurie blinked. "Size? Diapers come in sizes?"

Alexis shook his head. "They do. Do you know how old she is? How many months?"

"Candace didn't tell me. We broke up a little over a year ago, though, so I'm guessing three or four months old."

"I see." Alexis tilted his chin toward one of the diaper packs of the shelf. "That one should be fine."

Laurie grabbed it and looked at it. On the pack, there was a smiling baby. Melissa had been anything but smiling since Candace had dumped her with him, but at least right now, she was quiet. "So that's what the numbers in the corner are?"

"Exactly. How many packs do you need?"

"I don't know. Candace can buy her own diapers, right?"

Alexis looked at Laurie like he was an idiot. "She no doubt can, but you're going to need at least one pack for your place. That way, you don't have to run to the grocery store every time Candace leaves Melissa with you."

Laurie was horrified. "She's going to leave Melissa with me more than once?"

Alexis had to believe Laurie was an idiot by now. Laurie couldn't blame him. He felt like one, but he couldn't wrap his mind around everything that was happening. It was too much, all at once.

He didn't want to have a baby. He would do anything Candace wanted except that. He could sign away his rights, everything else, but not take care of Melissa.

"I don't know," Alexis said slowly. "Haven't the two of you talked about this?"

"Not really. She knocked on my door this morning, and I hadn't seen her for more than a year. She dumped Melissa into my arms, told me she was my daughter and that she would be back later, and left."

Alexis frowned and looked down at Melissa. "That doesn't sound right."

"That's what I've been saying all along," Laurie exclaimed. At least someone agreed with him.

"You're saying you didn't know you had a daughter until this morning?"

"I had no idea. Trust me. I've always made sure to be careful. I never wanted something like this to happen. I'm too young to have children."

"On that, we agree. I don't like that Melissa's mother did something like this, and even less that you don't know how to deal with a baby. What if you hurt her?"

That hurt Laurie more than it should have. It was a legitimate question. He'd never dealt with a baby, and even though he knew to support their heads and obviously not to drop them, that was where his knowledge ended. It had taken him two tries to change Melissa's diaper, which was why he was at the grocery store right now. He needed new diapers because he'd used up the ones that Candace had put in the bag.

He wouldn't even have known where to start to feed her. Alexis had made it look natural, as if he did this every day. Maybe he did. He had mentioned something about babysitting and studying to be a teacher. On the other hand, Laurie didn't know where to start, and it was a small miracle that he hadn't hurt Melissa yet.

He rubbed his face. "Well, I haven't hurt her, and I'll do my best not to. Candace said she'd be back tonight, and hopefully, Melissa won't cry again until then."

Alexis arched a brow. "You truly have no idea what you're in for, do you?"

"None of my brothers have children. Even if they did, I would never be asked to take care of them. I don't like kids. I don't want them."

Alexis's expression hardened. "Are you saying you're going to dump Melissa, too?"

"Not dump her." Even though that was what Laurie had been thinking about. He was nowhere near as good as Alexis at taking care of the baby, but it was more than that.

He was only nineteen. He had a crappy job and a crappy apartment. He was barely responsible for himself, let alone a baby. How was he supposed to give Melissa the life she deserved? He didn't understand why Candace had done this to him and why she hadn't told him about Melissa before today. If she'd been planning on keeping Melissa from him, why had she changed her mind? And if she hadn't been, why had she kept Melissa a secret until now?

Nothing in the situation made sense, and Laurie had no idea what to do.

"I've never understood how some people don't want their children, but I suppose I'm not you," Alexis said. He was looking at Melissa, and his expression shifted again. It was softer now, and it was clear he enjoyed taking care of the baby.

Laurie wished he could feel the same and that he could have the same ease, but he felt like if he touched Melissa, he was going to hurt her. Maybe Alexis wasn't wrong after all.

"I don't know what I want," Laurie admitted. He had no idea why, because he would never talk about this to a stranger, but he supposed that in a way, Alexis wasn't a stranger. He was Laurie's mate.

Laurie hated it.

"Well, it looks to me like you're going to have to make a decision about that," Alexis said, looking at Laurie again. "And about everything else, too."

Once again, Laurie wanted nothing more than to turn around and run away.

Alexis had said the wrong thing. One look at Laurie's face was enough to tell him that. He hadn't been able to ignore the fact that they were mates, though. Were they going to talk about it?

But instead of doing that, Laurie reached for Melissa. Thankfully, she was done eating, and Alexis allowed her father to take her.

"You need to burp her," he said.

Laurie blinked at him. "What does that mean?"

Alexis wasn't surprised he didn't know. Instead of answering, he opened the diaper bag again, taking out the towel he'd seen in there earlier. He put it on Laurie's shoulder, then helped him get Melissa into position. He could feel Laurie watching him, but he focused on the baby. It was much easier and more comfortable.

He gently patted Melissa's back. "You have to do this every time she eats. She might throw up a bit when she burps, but it's unavoidable." Thankfully, this time, she didn't.

She burped, startling Laurie, who looked at her with wide eyes. "That was loud for such a little baby."

It made Alexis laugh. "You haven't heard anything yet. But remember, every time she eats, you have to do that. And don't forget the towel. She might get baby puke all over you if you do, and I don't think you want that to happen."

Laurie looked horrified, but he nodded. "Thank you for the

tips." He hesitated. "And for everything else."

"When she cries, the first things to check are her diaper and whether it's time for her to eat. Usually, those two things will be enough to help a crying baby. If both of these things are okay, though, you're going to have to take a guess. With babies, it could be anything, so make sure she's warm enough but not too much and walk with her in your arms. That's often enough to get babies to stop crying." Alexis wanted to do much more, but he knew that the only thing he could do was give Laurie pointers and hope he would manage to deal with this.

"Thank you."

"And if anything happens, call her mother. She shouldn't have dumped Melissa with you without telling you what was going on and when it's clear you don't know what to do." Alexis leaned down and grabbed the diaper bag. He put the empty bottle into it, then hooked the bag around Laurie's shoulders. "But I'm sure your mother wouldn't mind helping you deal with Melissa if you need it."

Everyone knew about the Long family. Alexis had gone to school with Andy, one of Laurie's brothers. They'd never been friends, but they'd been friendly, and Alexis knew a lot about the seven brothers, enough to be sure that Laurie's mother would be over the moon happy at having a granddaughter.

His words made Laurie look horrified, though. "I'm not going to call my mom. She would kill me."

Right. Because Laurie had just found out that he was a father, so of course his family didn't know yet. Alexis grimaced at the thought of Laurie having to tell his mother. He knew how *his* mom would react to the news, and he could imagine Laurie's mother would take it pretty much the same way, at least in the beginning.

Laurie looked ready to bolt, and Alexis wanted to give him

the opportunity to do so. First, though, he had to say something about the elephant in the room. "I know you smelled it, too," he murmured.

He hadn't thought it possible, but Laurie looked even more frightened than before. He took a step back, almost hitting the shelves behind him. He was still juggling the diaper bag, Melissa, and the pack of diapers he had to buy, and Alexis expected him to drop something sooner rather than later. Hopefully, it wouldn't be Melissa.

"I don't know what you're talking about," Laurie said.

Alexis suppressed a sigh. "I know you're my mate, and I know you have to know I'm yours. That's how it works."

Laurie shook his head, and instead of answering, he turned around and walked away so quickly that he might as well have been running.

Alexis watched him go, knowing he couldn't go after him, no matter how much he wanted to. Obviously Laurie couldn't deal with them being mates in this state, and Alexis didn't blame him. He'd just found out he was a father and had found his mate in the same day. That would be enough to overwhelm anyone, let alone someone like Laurie. He was too young to have all these responsibilities, yet they were on his shoulders now, and he was going to have to make decisions that would change people's lives, and not only his.

Besides, Alexis didn't mind that Laurie didn't want to talk right now. It was a lot even for him to take in, and having Laurie walk away gave him time to think. Plus, he knew where Laurie worked. He could find him if he wanted to, and he knew that eventually, he would head over to the coffee shop and try to talk to him. Hopefully, not having Melissa with him would help. Alexis couldn't be sure of that, but he could be sure that going after Laurie right now would be the worst thing he could do, both for Laurie and for himself.

Instead, he grabbed his cart and went back to his grocery

shopping. He couldn't stop thinking about Laurie and Melissa, though. She was adorable and clearly was her father's daughter. Alexis couldn't help but wonder if that would be enough to get Laurie to welcome her into his life. He'd sounded like it was the last thing he wanted, and Alexis wouldn't be surprised if he decided to give up his rights. He hoped that wouldn't be the case. Melissa deserved to have her father in her life, and Alexis suspected that Laurie deserved to have his daughter, too.

He might be panicking and not have any idea what to do, but he'd been trying. It would have been easy for Laurie to take Melissa to his mother, even though his mom would have been angry. She would have taken care of the little girl, and Laurie would have been free to go along with his day and his life the way he wanted to. Instead, he'd kept Melissa with him, and he'd been trying hard. That endeared him to Alexis, and it was one of the things that had pushed Alexis to help him.

Alexis still didn't know what to think about the fact that they were mates, but there had to be a good reason for that. He wasn't sure he believed the thing about mates being perfect for you. There was no way Laurie was the perfect guy for him. They were too different, but Alexis couldn't deny what had happened. He'd smelled Laurie, and he was sure of it. They *were* mates.

Alexis hadn't expected to meet his mate this early, and he realized that Laurie and Melissa were probably a package deal at this point. That meant that as well as a mate, he would find himself with a stepdaughter, and while he loved the idea, he didn't know if he could add that to his life. He was already swamped.

He didn't have to make any of these decisions now. He had to allow Laurie to make his own, to decide whether or not he wanted to be in Melissa's life. Hopefully, it wouldn't take more than a few days, but Alexis wouldn't swear on that. It was a huge decision to make, especially because Laurie was so young. Finding each other complicated everything, but Alexis needed to keep faith and think as much as Laurie did.

Because meeting his mate didn't mean he had to be with him. They could ignore the bond and go their separate ways like Laurie had probably been planning. Alexis wouldn't let him go so easily, though. He might not know what to think about the situation, but he was sure of one thing—he wanted a clear answer when it came to him and Laurie. If Laurie was going to dump him, he would have to tell him to his face.

In the meantime, Alexis needed toilet paper.

CHAPTER THREE

Laurie was pissed by the time Candace came back to pick up Melissa in the early afternoon. It took everything he had not to blow up at her, even though he glared for all his might. She didn't seem impressed, though, and she barely looked at him as she walked into the apartment. She made a beeline for Melissa, holding her arms out as if she hadn't seen her for weeks rather than a day.

"How are you doing, baby?" she asked, taking Melissa from the floor where Laurie had placed her.

Alexis given Laurie, that tip, but Laurie had a phone, and he could Google like the best of them. Apparently, the floor was the safest place for a baby to be, since he didn't have a stroller or anything like that, so he'd stretched out a sheet and had placed the baby on that instead of holding her the entire day. It didn't look like it, but a baby got heavy after a bit. It was like holding a bag of sugar or two for the entire day. Laurie's arms were tired.

Laurie closed the door and crossed his arms over his chest. He waited for Candace to remember he existed, and when she did, he finally snapped. "What the fuck were you thinking?"

Candace's expression shifted from happiness to anger. "That you're her father and that you have responsibilities."

"And you only remembered that this morning? Because you never even told me you were pregnant, let alone that I had a daughter."

"Well, now you know."

"The best way to tell me I had a kid wasn't to dump her on

39

me without even telling me of her existence. You barely stayed long enough to make sure I wouldn't kill her this morning. You know I have no experience with children. What would have happened if I hadn't been able to deal with her?"

It had been a close call, and Laurie was pretty sure that if he hadn't met Alexis at the grocery store, things would have gone even worse. He was still panicking at the thought of having a child, and he still had no idea what to do about this entire situation, Alexis included.

Candace had the good taste to look ashamed, at least for a moment. Then, she straightened her back and looked straight at Laurie. "I thought you'd go to your mother. She raised seven children. Surely she could have helped you."

Laurie threw his hands in the air. "Maybe, after she killed me. What did you think I was going to tell her? *Hi, Mom, turns out I have a daughter, and I need your help with her*?"

"You're an adult. Why are you keeping secrets from your mother?"

Laurie arched a brow. "Are you telling me you told your mother that you were pregnant as soon as you had a positive test?"

Candace's cheeks flushed. "All right, maybe you have a point."

"At least you're admitting that," Laurie grumbled. He sighed and rubbed his face. He felt like he hadn't slept in a week, and he couldn't wrap his mind around how tiring it was to have to take care of a baby. Melissa had slept part of the morning, yet he hadn't been able to stop freaking out over everything. He wondered if he would be able to close his eyes and go to sleep tonight.

"I'm sorry, okay?" Candace said. She sat on the couch, smiling down at Melissa. "My mother was supposed to take care of her this morning, and I had a job interview. I couldn't find anyone else on such short notice when my mom told me she couldn't babysit."

"And you thought to bring her to me? It's a miracle I didn't kill her."

Candace narrowed her eyes. "I know that you've never had to deal with children, but surely even you aren't that stupid."

"It was a close thing a few times." Laurie sat on the couch next to Candace. "What happened? I haven't heard from you for close to a year, then suddenly, you reappear, and I have a daughter. You weren't planning on telling me or on having me be part of Melissa's life. What changed? Was it only that you needed a babysitter?"

Candace looked away again. "I'm sorry for the way I did this. You're right—I should have dealt with it differently. I panicked. I need this job, and I couldn't have gone through with the interview if Melissa had been with me."

"You didn't have to leave her with me the way you did, but fine. Let's move on from that. We've already decided that you fucked up, and I don't think we need to rehash that. Why didn't you tell me sooner?"

"I don't know. I honestly thought you'd want nothing to do with her. I guess I was afraid of rejection, not for me, but for her. What happens between us and how we deal with this isn't her fault, Laurie. She deserves to have both of her parents in her life, and I didn't know if you'd want to be."

Right now, Laurie felt he would be happier if he never saw Melissa again. He couldn't deny she was cute, though, and he was pretty sure Alexis would kill him if he gave up his parental rights.

Not that Alexis had a say in Laurie's life. They didn't know each other. Alexis had been nice at the grocery store, and he was Laurie's mate, but Laurie wasn't ready to touch that complication right now. He already had more than enough going on.

41

"I had no clue how to deal with her when she was born," Candace continued, her voice softer. "I had to learn everything, just like you did today."

"Your mother didn't help you?"

"Some. She said that Melissa was my responsibility, though. I'm the one who got pregnant, and I'm the one who decided to have the baby. She doesn't mind helping me, but I'm the mother. I think her words were that she wasn't about to parent another child, not at her age and when she wasn't the one who'd given birth."

Laurie couldn't say he blamed her. If he had a choice, he would run away screaming. Instead, he stayed right where he was on the couch.

"Unless you decide you want nothing to do with her, you have responsibilities, too," Candace continued. "Even though she wasn't planned, we created her together."

Laurie raked a hand through his hair. "This would have been easier to accept and to wrap my mind around if I'd known you were pregnant. You had nine months to get used to the idea of becoming a mother. You gave me five minutes to get used to the thought of being a father."

"I already apologized for the way I behaved. I was late and panicking."

"And I already said we didn't have to talk about that again. I still don't understand why you didn't come to me. Wouldn't it have been better for you to know for sure if I wanted to be her father *before* she was born?"

"What would you have done if I'd told you I was pregnant?"

Laurie didn't know how to answer that question. He had no idea.

Candace's tone was gentle as she continued, "I don't know for sure, of course, but I think that you would have done everything you could never to see me again. You'd have rejected both me and Melissa, and you wouldn't have given us a chance. Now that you know her, do you still want to stay out of her life?"

Laurie was tempted to say yes. It would make his life easier. He wouldn't have to tell his parents about Melissa or deal with the fallout of that. He could continue living his life with his crappy apartment and his crappy job, with no responsibilities.

He couldn't deny he was Melissa's father, though. That meant that whether he wanted it or not, he was responsible for her.

He sighed. "You're right. I'm her father, and I should act like it." Even though it was the most terrifying thing he'd ever done. "We need to talk about how we do things, though. You can't just dump her on me in the morning without telling me what's going on ever again. I could have needed to go to work. You're lucky it was my day off, and even luckier that you came now. My boss called me a few hours ago and asked me if I could take the evening shift." He hadn't made any promises, but he owed it to Roger.

"All right. I won't do that again. I really thought you'd tell your mother, though."

"I like my head where it is, thank you very much." Laurie bit his lower lip. "Where do we go from here, then?" He needed answers before he headed to work.

Then, he'd need the distraction of work.

Even though several hours had passed, Alexis still had no idea what to think about Laurie being his mate or how to deal with it.

Through Celine, he knew Laurie's reputation. He'd also seen it with his own two eyes as recently as the night before. He had no idea if Laurie had gone home with any of the girls he'd flirted with last night, and he wasn't going to ask, even when he saw Laurie again. Laurie wasn't one for commitment, yet being with your mate was the commitment of a lifetime. How was Laurie going to deal with that?

Would he deal with it at all?

Alexis wanted to go to the coffee shop to find Laurie, but he was pretty sure Laurie wouldn't be there today. He was with his daughter, and that took precedence over his job and Alexis. That was how it should be.

Maybe Alexis could go to the coffee shop anyway. If Laurie wasn't there, he would grab a coffee and go along with his day. If Laurie was there without Melissa, they might have a chance to talk. It was probably too soon, but Alexis didn't think he would be able to go on with his life without knowing at least that Melissa was okay. It would also be nice to know what Laurie was planning for their relationship, though.

They needed to talk. There was no way around that, and ignoring it wouldn't help. If anything, it would make the problem even bigger. Alexis didn't know what he wanted from his bond with Laurie, but he wouldn't find the answer by looking the other way. Hopefully, Laurie would understand that, and he wouldn't tell Alexis to fuck off.

Besides, Alexis was curious about Laurie, and he wanted to get to know him. So far, he didn't have a good impression, but he could admit that he barely knew his mate. Celine had talked about Laurie a lot when she'd had a crush on him, but Alexis doubted he could believe everything she'd said. He also didn't want to believe what he'd seen with his own two eyes. After all, that was the Laurie everyone saw. There had to be more to him than that, or at least, Alexis hoped so. They wouldn't be mates without a good reason, and he kept that in mind as he headed toward the coffee shop.

He'd never quite thought about when he'd meet his mate. A lot of shifters never did, and he'd imagined that eventually, he would meet a nice man, marry him, and they could have children. That was one thing he wasn't ready to give up, not even for his mate. He wanted kids eventually, and he wanted a man who agreed with that.

That seemed like it wouldn't be a problem if he and Laurie got together. Laurie already had a daughter, and while Alexis hadn't been planning on becoming a stepfather anytime soon, he wouldn't back down from the opportunity and challenge. He had to find out what Laurie wanted first, though.

That was going to be a challenge, too. If Laurie was anything like he showed the world — and there was a good chance he was — it would take him a while to wrap his mind around the fact that he couldn't flirt with half the town anymore. Alexis wanted to think Laurie would manage. He might not have the best impression of his mate for now, but he was going to give Laurie a chance.

The coffee shop was busy when Alexis got there, even though it was going on seven PM. Apparently it stayed open until ten, so Alexis would have the time to get a coffee and maybe even something light for dinner. The salads and sandwiches displayed in the glass cases looked good, but he decided to wait a bit longer in case Laurie was able to sit with him and talk. In the meantime, he sat at the table with his coffee and looked around.

The place was like he'd expected, which meant it was like every single coffee shop he'd ever been in. The counter was stacked with machines Alexis wouldn't be able to operate even if someone explained them to him, including a bean grinder that made a racket when the girl behind the counter used it. The chair he was sitting on was comfortable, though, and it felt a bit like home.

The scent of freshly brewed coffee and espresso was soothing. Maybe Alexis shouldn't have gotten a latte, since it would make it hard for him to fall asleep tonight, but he suspected he would have had a hard time anyway. He hadn't been able to stop thinking since he and Laurie had met at the grocery store, and he probably wouldn't be able to for a few days. Meeting your mate was a life-changing situation, even when your mate ran away from you.

Alexis took a sip of his latte. Like his sister always teased, it was more milk and sugar than coffee, but that was how he liked it. He didn't enjoy the bitterness of black coffee, and he wouldn't drink it even if he was forced. The coffee was good, though, and he briefly closed his eyes, trying to relax.

Whatever happened with Laurie, it didn't have to change anything.

Alexis wrapped his hands around the warm mug and tried to breathe. He hadn't wanted anything to do with Laurie as recently as yesterday, yet here he was, hoping Laurie would give him the time of day. The only thing that had changed was that now he knew they were mates. What if Laurie didn't want anything to do with Alexis, though?

Alexis would survive. He didn't need his mate, even though he wanted him by his side. He would eventually find someone else, maybe when it was more appropriate for him, after he was done with college and had found a good job.

He opened his eyes and blinked. He was here to see Laurie, so he probably should at least ask about him. So far, he hadn't noticed him anywhere, so maybe he was still with Melissa. Alexis hoped Melissa's mother had come back, but his stomach churned at the thought that she might not have. Would Laurie be okay if he had to keep Melissa for the night?

The back door opened, and Alexis turned his gaze toward it. He relaxed when he saw Laurie walk in. He was wearing an apron and looked like he'd been here for a while, so maybe he'd been on a break. Melissa wasn't with him, and Alexis hoped she was with her mother. He didn't know why the woman had decided that dumping her daughter on Laurie's doorstep was a good idea, but if Alexis ever met her, he would make sure to tell her what he thought about that. It might not be his business, but Melissa could have been in danger, and that wasn't something he could tolerate.

Laurie hadn't noticed him yet, and Alexis watched him, although since he didn't want to be obvious, he took out his phone and opened a book. He was used to seeing Laurie carefree, laughing and talking. Today, he was different. He wasn't smiling as much, and it was obvious there was something on his mind. Alexis wondered if it was him or Melissa, but it was probably a mix of the two.

He licked his lips. He'd come here to see Laurie, but he didn't actually have a plan in mind. He was flying blind, which probably wasn't the best idea, considering the situation. He had two options. He could wait for Laurie to notice him and see what happened, or he could try to sneak out before Laurie saw him. He would have to come back if he went that way, but maybe it wasn't such a bad idea. Maybe it would be better to put some time and distance between them before asking Laurie to talk.

Alexis was still trying to decide when Laurie turned and his eyes focused on him.

What the fuck was Alexis doing here? Laurie hadn't expected to see the man this soon after they'd met and realized they were mates, but maybe he should have. They'd only talked once, but Alexis hadn't seemed like the kind of guy who avoided complications, and that apparently included finding his mate.

Laurie rubbed his face. He didn't know if he could deal with this, not today. He didn't want to make a scene, so instead of going to Alexis and demanding an explanation like he was tempted to, he moved to the counter where Gemma was working. She looked up and smiled, and he smiled back. No one could resist a Gemma smile, not even him.

"I thought you were bringing back caramel syrup," she said.

That was what Laurie had been trying to find in the stockroom, but unfortunately, they were out. "I already told Roger he needed to get more. He said there's a shipment arriving tomorrow morning. In the meantime, you're going to have to use what you already have."

She grimaced. "Not going to be easy. A lot of people will be disappointed they can't get their caramel latte."

"I'll write a sign and put it up by the counter so they know, and you don't have to repeat it all the time." Chances were, they would have to anyway. Even though most people could read, a lot of customers tended not to or didn't believe the sign. Laurie always wanted to ask them why the fuck he would have written it if it wasn't true, but now more than ever, he needed this job.

"Thanks."

Gemma turned back to cleaning the coffee machine, and Laurie hesitated. He peeked at Alexis, who was still sitting in his chair, looking relaxed as he sipped his coffee. He wasn't staring at Laurie, something for which Laurie was thankful, but he was still there, and it was impossible for Laurie to ignore him.

"Hey, have you seen that guy?" he asked.

Gemma frowned. "What guy?"

"The one sitting there by the window? He's wearing jeans and a red t-shirt." And he looked delectable in it. Laurie had noticed that at the grocery store, but he'd been distracted by Melissa and the sound of his life crashing and burning. Alexis was attractive, and Laurie would feel lucky he'd snagged such a hot guy as his mate in any other circumstance.

Okay, maybe he wouldn't. He hadn't been planning on

meeting his mate, and he still didn't know what to do with Alexis or what he wanted. Still, it was kind of satisfying to know that his mate was so sexy and exactly the kind of guy he would choose for himself if he had to.

Gemma twisted and looked at Alexis. "Oh, him. There's nothing much to say. He came in, grabbed a latte with a lot of sugar, and sat down. Why? Do you know him?"

Laurie bit his lower lip. "Kind of."

Gemma arched a brow. "What does that mean?"

"I do know him. We're not friends, though."

"You look interested." Gemma leaned her hip against the counter and crossed her arms over her chest. "I don't blame you. He's hot."

"Contrary to what everyone says, I don't fuck everything that moves."

Gemma wiggled her eyebrows. "You usually stick to girls, but I've noticed you staring at guys, too. I never asked. I just assumed you were either bi or pan. Was I wrong?"

"No." But Alexis wasn't just a guy. Laurie couldn't explain that to Gemma, because she didn't know about shifters. She was human, just like everyone in the coffee shop. Well, everyone but Laurie and Alexis. There was also the Melissa complication. It was a lot to deal with, and Laurie was nowhere close to feeling okay.

He decided to ignore Alexis, at least for now. He'd been fucking around a lot on the job, knowing Roger wouldn't fire him, but now that he had Melissa, he needed to step up. He had no idea whether or not he would be a good father, but he was determined not to be a bad one. He hadn't wanted or planned Melissa, and he still panicked at the thought of being a dad, but it was either that or running away, and it was what everyone expected from him.

He'd prove them wrong.

He smiled at Gemma again. "I'm going back to the

stockroom. It needs to be cleaned."

Gemma shook her head. "You have to stay here. I need to leave in fifteen minutes."

Laurie groaned. "You mean I have to work the rest of the shift on my own?"

"Sorry. I thought Roger had told you."

"He knew I wouldn't come if he did."

So Laurie couldn't hide in the stockroom. That didn't mean he would have time to dedicate to Alexis, so he decided to do everything he could not to look at his mate and instead take care of the customers and the coffee shop. There was always more than enough to do, and after serving two teenage girls, he grabbed a rag and a bottle of cleaning spray and went to work on the counter.

He and Alexis ignored each other for a while. It helped Laurie relax, and by the time he looked up, an hour had passed. Alexis was still there, doing something on his phone. It was clear by now that he wasn't going anywhere and that he was probably waiting for Laurie to take the next step. Laurie could either continue the way he had or act like an adult for once.

He huffed and prepared a fresh coffee for Alexis. Chances were that he was done drinking the one he already had, and if he wasn't, it would be cold. He also got an espresso for himself. Then, after making sure everyone else in the shop was busy and didn't need anything, he made his way to Alexis's table.

"What are you doing here?" he asked as he slipped into the chair in front of Alexis. He set the coffees on the table, pushing Alexis's toward him.

Alexis blinked at him. He looked surprised to see Laurie, but he put his phone down right away and grabbed the fresh coffee. "Thank you. You didn't have to do that. How much do I owe you?"

Laurie waved Alexis's words away. "Don't worry about it. What are you doing here, though?" he asked again.

Alexis wrapped his hands around the mug and stared at Laurie. "Isn't it obvious?"

"I was hoping it was something else."

"You didn't actually think it was, though."

Laurie tilted his chin toward the phone that was now on the table. "What were you doing on your phone?" He wasn't quite ready to go to the point, and this was a good distraction.

Alexis relaxed in his chair. "Reading something for college."

"You said you were studying to be a teacher?"

"I am. I want to be a teacher one day." He tapped his fingertips on the table. "I'm here because I was curious."

Laurie groaned. "You're not going to let me dance around the topic, are you?"

"I can if you want, but I don't think we should."

He wasn't wrong. Knowing what they were up against, or rather, what Alexis wanted from their relationship, would help. Laurie wouldn't have to obsess over it or wonder what was going on. Even though he didn't want to face Alexis and the bond between them, it was probably better for everyone, including himself, to do it.

He drank half of his espresso to give himself courage. "All right. Let's talk about this, although I want you to know I'm not happy about it. I was planning on avoiding the topic and you for at least a week, probably more. I don't appreciate being forced to talk about it or to face you."

Alexis quirked a brow. "Does that mean I can't come to the coffee shop anymore?"

Laurie glared at him. "That's not what I said. Now go on. I'm listening. You said you were curious about me, so what do you want to know?"

Alexis didn't know where to start. He was pleased that Laurie had decided to talk to him. He'd expected Laurie to continue ignoring him for the rest of the evening and to have to go home hyped-up on coffee and with no answers. Instead, Laurie was facing the problem, which was a surprise, considering what Alexis knew about him.

"First of all, how's Melissa?" he asked.

Laurie's glare deepened. "What, you think I left her alone in my apartment?"

Alexis didn't want to admit it, but he'd wondered. He was pretty sure Laurie wouldn't do that, or at least, he wanted to give him the benefit of the doubt. "Did you?"

Laurie huffed. He looked much younger when he acted like this, but then, he *was* young. Nineteen was way too soon to find your mate, and even worse, to have a child.

"Candace picked her up earlier. I was lucky she did, because Roger asked me to take the evening shift today. Gemma had to leave."

Alexis had noticed the girl who had left earlier. "Did you and Candace have the opportunity to talk?"

"We did." Laurie settled against the back of his chair. "I yelled at her for not telling me about the pregnancy and dumping Melissa on me the way she did. She admitted it wasn't right, but she had a job interview, and her mother backed out of babysitting. She needed me to step up."

"There's stepping up, and there's what she did. It wasn't fair to you."

"I know. It also wasn't fair of her to keep the pregnancy to herself. I don't know what I would have done if she'd told me she was pregnant, and I'll never find out at this point. I'm disappointed, though. Candace had nine months to get used to the thought of becoming a mother. I only had minutes to wrap my mind around the fact that I have a daughter."

"Did it become easier as the day passed?"

Laurie shrugged. "I guess? The tips you gave me this morning helped. I also remembered I had a phone and that I could use Google." He rolled his eyes. "I really should have thought about that sooner."

"You were panicking. I'm not surprised you didn't." Alexis couldn't imagine living what Laurie was going through right now, and he felt sorry that Laurie had gotten the news about being a father the way he had.

When Mark was born, Alexis had had his parents show him how to take care of him. Mark wasn't his son, but it had been hard anyway. He'd also had the knowledge that he could step away from it anytime he wanted. His parents appreciated the babysitting, but they didn't demand it from him. They could find someone else if they needed to, but Laurie couldn't do the same. He was Melissa's father, and if he wanted to be a good dad, he would have to step up. It was a complicated situation, but it looked like Laurie was dealing with it.

"Taking care of Melissa wasn't what I expected," Laurie said.

"What did you decide, then?"

"I'm still not sure. I told Candace that if she wanted to leave Melissa with me, she had to tell me sooner than a few minutes before doing it."

"So you're going to take care of her again?"

Laurie sighed. "I'll be honest—I don't want to. I want to plug my ears and start screaming so I don't have to face any of this. But I can't avoid it. I'm Melissa's father, and she deserves me to act like it." His eyes glinted. "Plus, I can show my family that I'm not an idiot like they all think."

Alexis wasn't sure that last one was a good enough reason to decide to be a father, but if it gave Laurie the push he needed, maybe it was. As long as Laurie realized that Melissa needed him to be there for her and that she came first, he wouldn't point it out.

"So you're a dad," he said.

"It's still impossible for me to think about myself that way, but I guess." He looked at Alexis. "What does that make you?"

"I don't know," Alexis said cautiously. "I suppose it depends on what we decide to do."

"Well, we're mates. There's no avoiding that, either."

"There isn't, but I'm not Melissa. You don't owe me anything. If you decide this is too much for you, I can walk away and never come back."

Laurie rubbed his face. "I don't know what I want. I always thought that I didn't want to meet my mate. I don't like that someone or something I don't even know decided you were the best person for me. My entire family has been telling me I would change my mind when I met you for most of my life, though."

"And you don't want to admit they were right." The situation pointed to that, from what Laurie had said about his family.

"Never. I guess that what I'm trying to say is that even though my first instinct in this situation, too, is to run away, I'm not going to do it." He swallowed loudly. "Besides, I need help."

Alexis had expected that. He didn't like what Laurie was saying about not wanting a mate, but he could respect it. He had no idea where Laurie was going with the last bit, though. "What do you mean?"

"With Melissa. You're aware I don't know what I'm doing with her, but I agreed to be her father, and I need help with that. I don't know where to start, but you know a lot about babies. You could help me."

Alexis's first instinct was to say yes. He loved taking care of babies, and Melissa had been a doll at the grocery store once she stopped crying. Besides, if he and Laurie were going to be in each other's lives, Alexis might as well get used to Melissa now.

But *would* he and Alexis be in each other's lives? Alexis had no way to know, and he could tell that even Laurie had no idea. He wasn't going to demand an answer now, even though he wanted to. He hoped Laurie would eventually change his mind about trying to show his family they'd been wrong, but he didn't know Laurie. It was a possibility he would have to deal with if it arose.

For now, it hadn't. Alexis didn't want to get hurt, but he couldn't dismiss the possibility that he and Laurie would try to work things out. If they did, Melissa would be part of Alexis's life as much as she would be in Laurie's. Besides, he couldn't abandon Laurie to himself when it came to taking care of Melissa. Laurie had been lucky today because he hadn't had to deal with much more than a change of diaper and a bottle, but what would happen the first time he had to take care of her overnight?

Alexis sighed. He'd come to the coffee shop hoping to get answers, but instead, he had even more questions than before. "How about I give you my number," he said slowly.

"What for?" Laurie asked.

"So you can call me if you need anything with Melissa."

Laurie stared. "That's it? I can only use it when it has to do with Melissa?"

"No. You can use it whenever you want. I don't want to push you. I think you already have more than enough things to deal with right now."

Laurie snorted. "You could say that." He hesitated. "I don't want to give you false hope, but I also don't want to tell you I'll never want anything to do with you. I don't know what will happen. I have to focus on Melissa first."

Even though he barely knew Laurie, Alexis was proud of him for realizing that. "I agree. Do you want me to stay away from you? Apart from helping you with Melissa, of course."

Laurie shook his head, surprising Alexis. "It wouldn't be fair to you."

"I don't think we should think about being fair in this situation."

"What I meant is that while I can't make any promises when it comes to us being together, I also don't want to act as if we're not mates. No matter how much it scares me, it's something I have to face. I guess we could try texting and calling? That way, we can get to know each other but still take things slow while I deal with Melissa and my family." Laurie shuddered. "Let me tell you — I'm not looking forward to that. My mom is going to kill me, and my brothers will tease me endlessly."

Alexis could do that. It was more than he'd expected, and maybe more than he wanted. He couldn't deny Laurie was his mate, just like Laurie couldn't, but they both had a lot of thinking to do.

Alexis had thought he could never want to be with Laurie because Laurie was immature and because of his reputation. Now, he realized he hadn't given Laurie enough credit. He might have been acting like a teenager until recently, but the fact that he was nineteen didn't mean much. He'd stepped up to being a parent, especially a surprise one.

Alexis didn't know what would happen with Laurie, but he should give him a chance. After all, Laurie was showing him that he deserved it. Instead of running away like he'd admitted he wanted, he was facing the situation when it came to both Melissa and Alexis. That was the first step, and hopefully, many more would come after that.

Only the future would tell.

CHAPTER FOUR

Laurie needed to tell his parents about Melissa.

The thought of doing so was terrifying. His mother would be so angry her head would probably spin a hundred and eighty degrees. His father, on the other hand, would be disappointed, which was almost worse. He never yelled, never told Laurie how much of an idiot he'd been, but he looked at Laurie with those sad eyes that made Laurie want to do anything to fix things.

The problem was that in this case, there was nothing he could do. There was no denying that Melissa was his daughter, and he couldn't just step back and ignore her. That would make his parents even angrier and more disappointed, but even more than that, Laurie didn't *want* to do it. The situation was challenging, but he'd made his decision. He was going to try to be her father, and while he didn't know if he'd manage, he wasn't changing his mind, no matter what his parents said.

Candace was right. He was nineteen, and he should start acting like an adult. She wasn't the only one who'd said it, and while it had been easy to ignore it when it came to Gilbert — who'd been repeating it for years — Laurie couldn't do the same with Candace. She needed him to grow up, and it was time.

He stared at the house. He'd grown up here, and when he was a teenager, he couldn't wait to leave. He was the youngest of seven brothers, and it hadn't been easy, even though they all loved each other. Laurie had always felt like he was less and like his parents could have stopped after Andy, and it wouldn't have made a difference. He'd been the difficult child, spoiled yet not completely happy, even though he had pretty much the perfect family.

No matter how he felt about his family, he prayed he wasn't about to lose them. He needed his parents now more than ever, but the situation was a lose-lose one. No matter what happened, he couldn't deny Melissa, and he couldn't avoid telling his parents about her.

He sucked in a breath. He might as well go in. Hopefully, since it was early afternoon, none of his brothers would be there. He'd been tempted to call Gilbert and ask him to come along, but doing this on his own was the first step to being more mature. Besides, he still needed to tell Gilbert about Melissa. Gilbert was going to be pissed that Laurie had kept a secret from him — worried, but also probably happy. He loved babies and children almost as much as Alexis, which Laurie found weird, but then, he wasn't like them. He never would be, but he'd promised himself he would try, and he was.

He moved toward the house. His feet felt like he was treading in water, but he managed to climb the porch steps and quickly knock on the door. No one answered, but he pushed it open anyway, sticking his head in and calling out, "Anyone home?"

Something made noise in the kitchen, and his mother appeared a few moments later. Her eyes were wide, but she was smiling. "Laurie? What are you doing here?"

Laurie stepped in. He felt a pang of guilt at how delighted his mother was that he was home. He didn't come around enough, did he? "I just wanted to visit."

"You know you don't have to knock on the door before coming in. This is your home."

"Even though I haven't lived here in a year?"

"It'll always be your home and your brothers'."

Laurie wasn't sure that would still be the case after she

found out what he was here to tell her, but he smiled at her. No matter what happened, his mother loved him. She might tell him he was a dumbass and too young to have a child, but she wouldn't cast him out. It wasn't the kind of person she or Laurie's father were, and he counted on that.

He closed the door and followed his mother to the kitchen. She was talking a mile a minute, which made him smile. He promised himself that if he was allowed, he would come more often. It wouldn't be just for his benefit anyway. He and Candace were trying to work out visitation when it came to him and Melissa, and while it wasn't easy, it was also kind of exciting. Laurie could see Melissa grow up with her six uncles and loving grandparents. She would be happy here, and hopefully, in time, so would Laurie's parents.

He was pretty sure his brothers wouldn't care about Melissa, at least not the way their parents would. They would tease, and they'd probably think he was an idiot and too young, but they'd be supportive. Things always went like that with them. They wouldn't be angry, but then they didn't have a reason to be.

"So, what's going on?" Laurie's mother asked. "Do you want coffee? I made a fresh pot an hour ago."

Laurie settled on the other side of the counter. He rubbed his palms on his thighs, wondering if this was the right moment to tell her. He was pretty sure there was no right moment, not for something like this. "No, thank you. I have to go to work for the evening shift later."

She nodded and turned to face him. "Not that I'm not happy to see you, but I can see something is going on. What is it?" She hesitated. "Is it your girlfriend? What was her name?"

"Natalie, but no, it's not." Laurie swallowed. "Actually, it's one of my older girlfriends, Candace. I don't know if you remember her."

"You were with her for a few months, weren't you?" Laurie's mother smiled. "Almost enough for us to meet her."

"Yeah, well, you're going to meet her eventually."

"You're back with her?"

This was it. Laurie was about to tell his mother that she was a grandmother, and he was freaking out. He couldn't look at her as he explained, "We're not. But we're going to be in each other's lives for a long time because she had a baby."

Laurie's mother was silent, and Laurie *had* to look at her. She was frowning as if she didn't understand, and Laurie was pretty sure he'd fucked it up.

"What do you mean?" Laurie's mother asked slowly.

Why was this so hard? "Candace and I had a baby. You're a grandmother. Her name is Melissa, and she's four months old."

Laurie's mother continued staring at him. He was waiting for an explosion, and sure enough, it came.

"You're telling me you have a *child*?"

Laurie raised his hands. "I would have told you sooner if I'd known, but Candace kept it a secret from me until last week. I had no idea she was pregnant, and I swear we were careful. I don't know what happened, but we're thinking a broken condom."

"*A broken condom?* Are you serious, Laurie? You're telling me you have a child at nineteen years old?" She shook her head. "How could you be so irresponsible? Does Candace even know you're a shifter and that her daughter could be one, too?"

Shit. Laurie hadn't thought about that. "Not yet, but Melissa is still young. There's time before she starts shifting."

"You don't know that! Do you ever *think* before you do things?"

It hurt. Laurie had expected it, and he'd known his mother would say things she would probably regret eventually. He deserved it, even though he would rather not hear it coming from his mom. "I promise you that I'll tell Candace about it. And I stepped up. I met Melissa, and she's really cute."

Laurie's mother took a step back. "Babies aren't just cute. They're a lot of work, work you're not used to doing. You haven't been doing anything with your life until now. How can you be a father?"

"There's no changing that I am, Mom. I already agreed to help Candace as much as I can, and Melissa *is* my daughter." Standing up to his mother was the scariest thing Laurie had ever done, but this was important. Maybe he could smooth things out a bit, though. "And I'm not doing this on my own."

"Of course not. Your daughter has a mother."

"She does, but that's not what I was talking about. I met my mate the same day I found out about Melissa, and he's been helping me. He's a great babysitter, and he's studying to be a teacher." That ought to help Laurie's mother accept things, right?

She stared at him. "You met your mate?"

"His name is Alexis. I know what I said about not wanting a mate, and I'm still not sure about it, but we're working things out between us, too. He knows Melissa comes first. He understands."

"He understands," Laurie's mother said slowly.

Laurie sighed. He was pretty sure he was going to have to answer about a hundred questions, and while he wasn't ready, there was no way out of it. "He does. Let me tell you about him and Melissa. I know you're angry, but this is the situation, and the only way to go about it is to accept it." Even though Laurie himself hadn't quite done it yet.

Alexis stared at his phone. So far, Laurie had never called him, which made him suspicious that he was now. Usually they stuck to texts, which made it easier for both of them. They could answer whenever they wanted, and Alexis was more comfortable with texts than phone calls anyway. Something had to have happened for Laurie to be calling, and since Alexis had no idea if it had to do with Melissa, he couldn't *not* answer.

"Hello?"

Laurie sighed heavily. "Thank God you answered. I need your help."

So it did have to do with Melissa. That was the only reason Alexis could think of Laurie needing him.

Not that he was bitter. Melissa came first, and he and Laurie had agreed to take things slow between them. Still, sometimes he was angry. He wasn't just a guy. He was Laurie's mate, and he deserved more than a few texts. This was what he'd agreed to, though, and he needed to deal with it. He'd also agreed to help Laurie as much as he could, so he'd better find out what Laurie needed. "What is it?" he asked.

"Can I see you?"

"Now?"

"Yeah. Or are you in class?"

"I'm home." For once, Alexis wasn't babysitting his brother, and he was thankful. Ever since he'd met Laurie, he felt like he wasn't quite steady on his feet, and he needed some time to wrap his mind around everything. His mother had noticed something was going on, but she hadn't asked, and Alexis hadn't volunteered information. He needed to know what was going on between him and Laurie before he did. He didn't want to make his mother happy only to yank that happiness away from her.

"Okay, great. I'm headed to the coffee shop. My shift starts in an hour, so we can talk a bit before then. Coffee's on me."

Alexis blinked. "The situation has to be dire for you to offer me free coffee."

"I offered you coffee last week, too."

When they'd talked about what being mates meant to them. Alexis remembered that moment, and he didn't think he would ever forget it. He still had no idea where his life was going, but that had been a crucial moment in it.

"I'll be there as soon as I can," he promised.

As he got ready to go out, he couldn't help but wonder what was going on. Laurie had sounded slightly panicky, but then, he often did when it came to Melissa. He and Alexis had seen each other twice since last week, and both times, Laurie had needed help with the baby. Apparently, Candace had gotten the job she'd interviewed for, and she needed a more reliable babysitter than her mother. The woman was more than happy to babysit the baby every so often, but not every day. That meant that Candace and Laurie were making things work around their schedules, and Laurie had to take care of Melissa more often than he'd expected and always on his own.

The first time she'd thrown up, he'd freaked out, and Alexis had arrived at his apartment to find him covered with vomit almost from head to toe.

The memory made Alexis smile. Even though he'd clearly been uncomfortable and disgusted, Laurie had still been trying to help his daughter. It had taken Alexis a while to reassure him that it was perfectly normal and that Melissa had probably swallowed more air than usual when he'd fed her. Laurie had been ready to take her to the hospital, but in the end, he'd listened to Alexis, and they'd spent the rest of the evening together. It had been nice and cozy, and it had given Alexis a glimpse of what their future would be like.

He hoped he wasn't wrong.

Laurie was already there when Alexis arrived at the coffee shop. He had two coffees in front of him at the table in the corner, and he waved when he saw Alexis. He was on his own, but that didn't mean this didn't have anything to do with Melissa. Every time they talked, Melissa was the main topic of their conversation.

Alexis slid into the seat in front of Laurie's and accepted his coffee with a grateful smile. He took a sip, then tried to relax. "What's going on, then?"

Laurie rubbed the back of his neck, which Alexis was learning was a sign that he was embarrassed and had probably done something he shouldn't have, like that one time he'd microwaved the wet wipes because he'd thought they were too cold for Melissa's bum.

"I told my parents about Melissa," Laurie said. "Well, my mom. My dad wasn't home, but I have no doubt he already knows. I'll have to go back to talk to him."

"How did your mother take it?"

Laurie grimaced. "As well as I expected, which is not well at all. She thinks I'm an idiot. She told me so."

"That was only her first reaction. She knows you're trying to do the right thing, but also how hard it is to have a child, and you're only nineteen. I don't think she wanted this for you, but she'll come around to it." Or at least, Alexis hoped so. It would be easier if Laurie had his family to back him up and help him.

"She kind of did, a bit." Laurie hesitated. "I told her about you, too."

So this was what Laurie had been hiding. "What did you say?"

"That I met my mate. That you're a great babysitter and that you're studying to become a teacher."

"That's it?"

Laurie huffed. "No. I also told her we were together."

Alexis briefly closed his eyes. "As in, that we're already a couple?" Alexis should have expected something like this.

"Yeah. I didn't mean to, but she was saying I wouldn't be

able to take care of Melissa on my own. I told her about you, and she thought we were together. I guess I didn't tell her that wasn't the case. Besides, you *are* helping me with Melissa."

"That's doesn't give you the right to lie about me. What's going to happen if you decide that you don't want to be with me after all? You'll tell your mother we broke up? How do you think she's going to take that?"

Alexis was angry. He understood why Laurie had lied and that he hadn't been planning to. His mother had assumed they were together, and he hadn't told her that wasn't the case. It was a lie by omission, but it still hurt. It pulled Alexis into the situation even though Alexis hadn't been sure about it, and now there was no easy way out for him.

Laurie leaned forward. "Please. Just listen, okay? I promise I didn't mean to do this. I panicked when my mother told me I was irresponsible, and it was the wrong thing to do." He chuckled darkly. "I realize this is the story of my life. You have to be angry to be stuck with me as your mate."

"I'm not angry. I'm disappointed and worried. We still don't know what's going to happen between us, and you shouldn't have lied to your mother. I don't like lies, Laurie. That goes for her, but it also goes for me."

"I swear I won't do it again. And I'm not planning on pushing you away."

It took Alexis a moment to remember what he'd said about that. "Even if you're not planning to do it, it doesn't mean you won't do it at all. I know what you think about mates. You're the one who told me you didn't like the idea of someone you didn't choose. What's to tell me you're not going to kick me out of your life once you don't need my help anymore?" And it would hurt. Alexis loved Melissa and taking care of her, and he was already starting to fall in love with Laurie.

He'd been telling himself not to, but it was no use. It really was true that his mate was perfect for him, and he loved

Laurie's determination—the way he faced his fears and admitted his downfalls. Those things wouldn't be enough to save them as a couple, though, not unless they were clear with each other.

"I fucked up." Laurie didn't want Alexis to think he would dismiss him as soon as he didn't need him anymore. He didn't understand why Alexis thought that, but he supposed that since Laurie knew Alexis's sister, Alexis might have heard it from her. Laurie had never cared about his reputation, but maybe he should have.

"You did. How are you going to fix this?" Alexis asked.

For a moment, Laurie had expected Alexis to leave, and he'd been terrified. He didn't want to lose Alexis, and not just because Alexis helped him with Melissa and had taught him everything he knew so far about babies—which wasn't a lot. Laurie would have been entirely lost without Alexis in his life, and it gave him a jolt to realize that.

But it was more. It was the time Alexis had stayed with Laurie even after Candace had picked up Melissa. They'd cleaned up the living room, which always looked like a tornado had come through after Melissa left. He'd even bought Laurie dinner when he'd realize how exhausted Laurie was, and he'd taken care of him the way he took care of Melissa. It had made Laurie feel less alone, and even though he still didn't know what to think about having found his mate, he couldn't deny he liked Alexis.

He didn't want to lose him.

Laurie swallowed. "I realize I need to grow up and change," he said slowly. "Until now, I behaved like I didn't have a care in the world, and that's because I didn't. I only had to think about my job and making enough money to pay rent. That was it. Now, though, I have a mate and a child, and

I want to do things the right way. It's only been one week, though. I don't think I can change that much in such a short time, no matter how hard I try. I'm sorry if I offended you, and I realize I shouldn't have lied, not even by omission. I just have no idea what I'm doing, and sometimes, I'm going to fuck up, both when it comes to Melissa and with you."

Alexis sighed and rubbed his eyes. "You're right. I apologize. I should have given you the benefit of the doubt before getting angry, and I should have tried to put myself in your position. I keep forgetting that you've only known about Melissa for a week."

Laurie snorted. "There's no way I'm forgetting that, trust me."

"You have things pretty much in hand with Melissa, though. You and she are going to be okay."

Alexis sounded convinced, and Laurie found himself hoping he was right. He wanted things to be okay with his daughter. She was still a baby, but he was planning on being in her life for a long time, no matter what it took.

Every time he had to take care of her, he found himself falling for her a bit deeper. In the beginning, she'd just been a bother. He'd been afraid to break her, and he still was, but now, he'd started seeing more. He loved playing with her and making her laugh, and he wanted more of that. He wanted more of being with her, but also with Alexis.

In the past week, when Alexis had come over to the apartment to help, they'd almost felt like a family. It had freaked Laurie out, and it still did. He'd always been anxious about the mate thing. He'd never wanted anyone or anything but him to decide who he would be with, but apparently, that wouldn't be the case when it came to Alexis. They hadn't kissed yet, but Laurie had thought about it, and he wanted to do it. He didn't want to complicate the situation, though.

He needed help. He didn't want to only need Alexis for

that, and he didn't, but how could he make Alexis understand that?

"We agreed to take things slow," he said, not sure where he was going.

"We did," Alexis confirmed. "That doesn't mean you can't change your mind."

"Or that you can't. Maybe you'll start to feel like having to deal with me and Melissa is too much for you. I would understand. I'm not going to college, but I can imagine that you barely have time for yourself between that and your job. Having a mate and a child makes things even worse."

"I'm not going anywhere."

Alexis's expression was so fierce that Laurie believed that. He realized he *wanted* to believe it. He needed Alexis for Melissa, but not only because of that. He liked Alexis, and while he still had doubts, now that they were spending time together, he understood that those doubts didn't mean anything.

He would have chosen Alexis for himself even if Alexis hadn't been his mate. He didn't know if they would ever have met, but if they had, he would have fallen head over heels in love with him. As it was, he was headed that way.

"That's good to know," he said, his mouth dry. "But I think we've been taking things maybe too slowly. I realize this isn't the right moment for us to get together, considering Melissa, but I don't spend all of my days with her. Maybe we could go on a date?"

"I don't understand. Last week, you didn't like the fact that you had a mate. Now you're asking me on a date?"

"The thing about mates didn't have anything to do with you as a person. I already explained that I disliked the thought of something choosing you for me. But after getting to know you, I realized that I would have chosen you for myself anyway, so what difference does it make? Besides, I'm pretty sure that the reason I hated the thought of mates so much is that I wanted to be contrary to my family. After the first time I explained my problem with it, they kept teasing me that I would change my mind once I met you. I decided I wouldn't let them win, but they were right." And it hurt to admit it.

Alexis shook his head. "I don't understand that thing you have going on with your family. It's almost as if you want to prove them wrong on everything, even when they're not."

Laurie shrugged. "It's exactly like that. I'm the baby of the family. I've always been coddled and teased, and I've always hated it. I don't want to be looked at as a child, not anymore."

"Then maybe stop acting like one. Doing things just because you know it goes against them is not the way to do that."

"I know!" Laurie sucked in a breath. "And I know I was wrong when it comes to the mate thing." Even though it was hard to admit, and not just because of his family. Laurie had to focus on Alexis as a person. He liked what he was getting to know, and he wanted more. "Will you go on that date with me?"

Alexis stared for a moment, and Laurie was convinced he would say no. When he nodded, Laurie could have kissed him. He was tempted to do just that, but he didn't want their first kiss to be in the middle of the coffee shop.

"I'll go on a date with you. I'm not sure when I'll be available, though."

"We can work something out," Laurie rushed to say. "And if it makes you uncomfortable to have to help me with Melissa for free, I can pay you for that work. I realize I should have offered sooner, but I didn't think about it. I want to do this the right way, Alexis, both when it comes to you and Melissa. I don't know what the right way is, though, which might become a problem, but I promise I'm trying as hard as I can."

Laurie didn't think there was anything else he could do, but he would find out if there was, and he would do it.

Laurie was trying, and in Alexis's opinion, that was all that mattered. He was still wary, but he was glad to see that at least Laurie had admitted he needed to change things. Alexis still didn't want to get his hopes up, even though Laurie had just asked him on a date, but he suspected that would change eventually.

What wouldn't change was that he didn't want to get paid to help Laurie, not when he hoped that in the future, he and Laurie would be together, and along with Melissa, they would be a family.

"I don't want you to pay me," he said.

Laurie looked relieved, which didn't surprise Alexis. It probably would have been hard for him to find the money. There was no way he made a lot here at the coffee shop. Alexis suspected that he would have done everything he could to find that money if Alexis had agreed to it, though.

"Are you sure?" Laurie asked.

"I'm sure. I'm not a babysitter, not to you."

"You're right. You're so much more than a babysitter, and I'm extremely grateful for everything you've done. I know it hasn't been fair to you."

Alexis shook his head. "Let's not talk about fairness. We're both dealing with the situation as best as we can, and in your case, you needed help I was more than happy to provide. But I'm your mate, and I don't want to be paid to babysit a girl that I hope eventually will become my stepdaughter." Alexis needed to say that. He wanted Laurie to see how serious he was.

Laurie paled a bit. "That's right. I hadn't thought about the situation from your point of view. Is that something you want, then?"

"I've always wanted children. I didn't think I would have one this soon, but I understand that being with you means having Melissa in my life, too. I don't have anything against that. She's a sweetie, and I enjoy spending time with her."

Laurie puffed up his chest a bit, just like any proud father, which made Alexis smile. "She *is* lovely."

"She is," Alexis agreed. "And I'm ready to teach you everything I can about how to deal with the baby and what you can expect. I'll also help every time I'm available, but you have to remember I also have a job and that I'm going to college."

"I won't forget that. But sometimes, I wonder if you're disappointed."

Alexis blinked. "About what?" He couldn't think of one thing in his life that had disappointed him recently.

"About me. I'm sure you had other plans when it comes to your mate or even just the person you'd spend the rest of your life with. Now here you are, saddled with me, a barely grown-up man who's freaking out about finding out he has a daughter, and of course, said daughter. I wouldn't have blamed you if you'd run away. I still wouldn't. I realize this wasn't part of your plans."

So far, Alexis and Laurie had barely touched. Alexis wanted to be sure it wouldn't make Laurie uncomfortable, and even when the occasion had arisen for them to be closer, Alexis had kept his distance. He didn't want to send Laurie running, which was bound to happen if he pushed too hard too fast. Right now, Laurie needed to be reassured, and Alexis reached out to take one of his hands.

He paused, expecting Laurie to pull away, but instead, Laurie twisted his hands so he could link their fingers together. Alexis's heart raced, but he found himself smiling.

"I'm not disappointed," he explained. "I'll admit I wasn't

sure what to do with you in the beginning, and sometimes, I still am because we have to find a way to fit our lives together, and so far, we haven't really managed. We haven't tried, either, though, and I'm sure that things will be better when we do. But you're my mate, Laurie, which means you're the most perfect person in the world for me. It might not feel like it to you right now, but once we settle down, I'm sure you'll realize that's the case."

"That's not what I was saying. I know I'm an idiot. I had no plans for my life until recently. I just wanted to continue working here as little as I could, make just enough money to pay rent and my bills, and coast along in life. I didn't have any dreams."

"But now you do?"

Laurie smiled deprecatingly. "Kind of, and I can't believe it's me thinking that. But I have to take care of Melissa, and I want to make you and her proud. My parents, too, although I suspect that's going to be harder. I don't want to be a kid anymore. I can't afford to, no matter how much I want it. My life was so much easier when I didn't have responsibilities."

"But you did have responsibilities," Alexis pointed out. "Even before, you had to come to work and pay your bills and rent. You managed to do that, which means you were responsible in a way."

"But not enough. Things need to change, and I've been working hard toward that."

"I know." And even though Alexis was still hesitant, he would give Laurie the benefit of the doubt. It was the only way they could move forward. "But I promise I'm not disappointed. I realize that not everyone can be like me and know what they want to do with their life as teenagers. I've always loved children and known I wanted to be a teacher, so it was easy for me to choose to go to college and to babysit on the side to earn enough money."

Laurie wrinkled his nose. "Do you, though? I'm not trying to offend you, but babysitting doesn't sound like it's something that will earn you a lot of money."

"My parents still help me when it comes to college, of course, but for the rest, I do manage. It would be easier if I had a roommate, but my old one moved out a few months ago, and I haven't been able to find a new one yet. But I promise you I'm doing okay. I babysit several children, and their parents are pleased with my work. That includes my parents, by the way. They've always made it clear that they would pay me if I agreed to babysit for them, and they do."

All of this was a lot to take in. Alexis still expected Laurie to run away, and he knew that eventually, Laurie would have to go to work. Right now, though, it felt like the perfect moment. They were still holding hands, and while Laurie seemed preoccupied, it made sense. He was worried about his daughter and their life, and while Alexis wanted to fix this for him, he knew it was something Laurie needed to figure out on his own.

"So we agreed to go on a date," Laurie said slowly.

"We should put our heads together and decide when we'll go. I know you have Melissa a lot of the time when Candace works, and I'm not sure what your schedule is when it comes to work."

Laurie groaned. "This was never a problem before. God, I hate being a responsible adult."

That made Alexis laugh. "I'm pretty sure most people feel that way. I sometimes do, too. I wish I could stay at home on the couch and watch Netflix instead of babysitting the kids at least a few times a week, but we do what we have to do, which in your case is dealing with your job, your daughter, and your mate." The last thing Alexis wanted was to push Laurie too hard, but he had to take a chance.

Thankfully, Laurie smiled. "You're right. It's part of being an adult, and it's what I am."

Alexis nodded. "And we don't have to pick a day now. We don't even have to go out for that date if you don't feel up to it or if you can't. As long as we spend time together, I'll be happy with that." Alexis had always been happier at home anyway. Having his mate stay with him would be even better, but the ball was in Laurie's court.

For once, Alexis couldn't wait to see what happened next and what Laurie came up with.

CHAPTER FIVE

"You've got this," Alexis murmured.

Laurie wasn't sure he was right. "Maybe you should do it."

"You need to learn how to do this, Laurie. It's not that complicated."

It was easy for Alexis to say that. He had experience, while Laurie had no idea what to do. "Why did Candace have to forget to get Melissa's bottles ready?" he asked with a groan.

Usually, Candace packed the formula already measured. Laurie only had to heat the water, mix everything, and give it to Melissa. Even though it was simple, he was always terrified of making a mistake. It was one of the reasons why when Alexis was at home with him, he was always the one making the bottles. He wasn't going to today, though.

"What if I put too much formula in the bottle?" Laurie asked.

"It won't change anything. Besides, it's not that hard to measure it. Open the tub. You'll see that inside of the container, there's a measuring spoon. You just have to use that."

They were standing in Laurie's kitchen, both of them staring at the tub of formula Laurie had bought for his apartment. So far, he hadn't needed to use it, since Candace had been good about sending Melissa to him with everything she would need. But the last time she'd been here, she'd seen the diaper packs and the formula Laurie had bought, just in case, and she'd seemed pleased. Laurie hadn't understood why until she arrived today, and Melissa's bag only contained a few diapers and nothing else. When he'd texted Candace to ask what had happened, she'd said that since he had everything Melissa would need at his apartment, she didn't need to fill up the diaper bag anymore.

She wasn't wrong, but it made Laurie freak out a bit, and not just because the formula hadn't been measured. The fact that he was keeping some of Melissa's things in his apartment meant she was becoming a part of his life, something he hadn't expected. He'd thought things would be awkward forever and that eventually Candace would decide he wasn't a good father and that he shouldn't get to spend time with Melissa. Instead, she was giving him Melissa more and more often, and while it pleased him, it also scared him.

Then there was Alexis.

He was always there when Laurie needed him. He'd recently started coming over every evening when Melissa was at Laurie's apartment, even when Laurie didn't call him for help. He seemed to enjoy spending time with the baby and Laurie, which created another kind of fear in Laurie.

He reached for the formula with trembling fingers and opened it. If he focused on doing this, he wouldn't have to think about Alexis and what they were to each other.

He had a hard time dealing with, well, everything. Laurie could admit that, at least to himself. Now that things were settling down with Melissa, he had more time to obsess over Alexis.

In the beginning, he'd gone along with the situation because it was the easiest thing to do. He needed Alexis, and he wanted him in his life. He still hadn't come to terms with the fact that he'd found his mate, though.

He'd always thought that if he met his mate, he would reject them. In part, it would have been because he wanted to show his family that he wouldn't allow anyone, not even fate or whatever chose mates, to dictate how we should live his life. In truth, he was uncomfortable with the thought of being with someone he was *supposed* to be with. Yes, he would have chosen Alexis himself if he'd had the opportunity, but he hadn't had it.

Laurie disliked not having complete control of his life. He'd done everything he could to have it, yet here he was, with a daughter he hadn't planned on having and a mate he didn't know how to deal with.

It wasn't just because he and Alexis were mates, though. They worked well together. Alexis was a great friend, and Laurie liked him. Alexis was also great with Melissa, which made Laurie's heart feel strange every time he watched them together.

And that was the problem, wasn't it? Laurie was used to short relationships—if he could even call them that. Being with someone for a few weeks wasn't a relationship. He had no idea how to behave with someone he wanted to be with for the long term, and just thinking about being with someone for years, even decades, made him want to run to his closet and hide inside. How was he supposed to make Alexis love him? He was a mess, and he felt like he always would be.

"I can do it if you want," Alexis suddenly said.

Laurie realized he'd been standing there holding the formula and not doing anything with it. So far, Melissa wasn't crying, but it was going to happen sooner rather than later, because it was time for her bottle. As it was, she was staring at Laurie from Alexis's arms and sucking on her fist, drooling everywhere.

Laurie had to stop being an idiot. It wouldn't be easy, because he always felt like one, but he knew he could do this. In this situation, getting a baby bottle ready was the easiest thing he could do.

"I'll do it," Laurie said. He looked inside the tub, and sure enough, the measuring spoon was right there. He made sure to fill the bottle just so with boiling water, then added the formula and mixed everything. It was still hot, so he left the bottle on the counter and turned to Alexis.

He was looking at Laurie with a proud expression Laurie was pretty sure he didn't deserve.

"I know why you have to make the formula with boiling water, but it doesn't make sense," he said in a rush. He wasn't ready to face whatever Alexis was feeling.

Alexis frowned. "What do you mean?"

"You know how Melissa gets when she's hungry. She starts screaming, and you have to get her food as soon as possible. How can you do that if you used boiling water? You're going to have to wait for the milk to cool down, and she's going to scream the entire time."

For some reason, that made Alexis smile. "You're not wrong, but there's no way out of this. That's why it's good for you to learn the signs that Melissa is getting hungry. You can get the bottle ready a bit sooner, and once she starts crying, it'll be perfect. You still have to check the temperature, though."

Laurie rolled his eyes. "I know. I've been doing it since I first had to take care of her." Because he'd seen Alexis do it at the grocery store. He wouldn't have known it was a thing if he hadn't, and he shuddered when he thought about the consequences it could have had for Melissa. Candace really hadn't been thinking that day, because if she had, she would have known how bad an idea it was to leave her daughter with Laurie.

That was in the past, though, and Laurie had been getting better at taking care of his daughter. He had to, because his mother refused to help him. She was still angry, and even though that didn't mean she wouldn't answer his phone calls, she'd been clear that Laurie would have to do this on his own. He'd made a mistake, and he had to deal with the consequences.

Thankfully, Laurie had Alexis. He also had Candace, and even his brothers and his father—and Gilbert. He'd laughed for about ten minutes when Laurie had told him about Melissa, but he was already a dotting uncle. All of Laurie's brothers had called, some to tease him, some to ask what had happened. Everyone had been supportive. Laurie's father had clearly been disappointed, but he also sounded proud that Laurie was stepping up, admitting his mistakes, and learning how to be a dad. Laurie hadn't expected any of this, and it confused him. He'd spent so much time trying to stay away from his brothers that he hadn't realized how much they cared about him.

Melissa cried out, and Alexis rubbed her back to shush her. Laurie grabbed the bottle to check the temperature, and since it had cooled enough, he handed it to Alexis. Alexis took it with a smile and moved Melissa into the right position, then popped the bottle into her mouth and headed toward the couch.

Laurie watched him go. He'd never imagined his life would be like this, with a daughter and a mate. This was nothing like he'd expected, but then, he hadn't expected much of himself. It was strange, but he couldn't deny that even though it was nothing like he'd thought his life would be, he liked it.

Very much so.

Laurie was overthinking things today, and Alexis wasn't sure why. He'd decided to give Laurie space, and hopefully, it would be enough for him to deal with his feelings and find a solution for whatever was making him nervous.

He settled on the couch, smiling as Melissa drank her milk. It was a familiar position, but the feelings were different than any other time he'd done this because of Melissa and who she was. She wasn't just a kid that Alexis was babysitting. She wasn't even Alexis's brother. Technically, Alexis wasn't much of anything to her except a babysitter, but he already viewed her as his daughter.

This wasn't how his life was supposed to go.

He'd planned everything because he was a planner, and he was panicky when things didn't go the way they should have. He hadn't expected to meet his mate this young, but he supposed that even if he had, he could have gone ahead with all his plans. But his mate came with a baby, which put an even bigger wrench into Alexis's carefully planned life.

But he couldn't ignore Laurie and Melissa, and he didn't even want to try. It didn't matter that he was only twenty-four and that he wasn't done with his degree yet. He could do this, and so could Laurie.

And Laurie *was* doing it. Sometimes, just like he had with the formula, he lost himself in the details he shouldn't have a problem with, but Alexis realized it was because he was so out of his depth. Once he stopped obsessing over the details, he was a great father, and he was becoming better day after day. Alexis could see Laurie truly becoming the dad Melissa deserved, and it pleased him.

What didn't please him was the fact that while Laurie was great at being a dad, they were still awkward at being a couple. He wasn't even sure they were a couple at all, to be honest. They were mates, but they were always so focused on Melissa that it was hard to find the time and space to be together. They hadn't gone on that date yet, and Alexis didn't know if they would. He couldn't even blame Laurie for not pushing. Between both their schedules and Melissa, they just didn't have time to go out without the baby.

There was also the fact that while Alexis was still hesitant, Laurie was skittish. He seemed to scare himself every time he reached for Alexis, and he always snatched his hands away, as if he was afraid that Alexis would reject him or that something he didn't want to happen would. He'd said that he wanted to see where things would go, but it looked like he was still terrified of having found his mate to Alexis.

Alexis couldn't blame him. He was terrified, too. Meeting his mate wasn't part of his plan, but he was learning to deal with it since he had. Thankfully, so was Laurie. Alexis hoped that eventually, they would work as a couple. They had time, after all, and it didn't matter if it took them a year or even more to find their footing. If anything, Alexis's mother would be more comfortable with that. She hadn't tried to keep Alexis away from Laurie and Melissa, but she'd been wary of him taking on even more responsibilities.

"Candace is going to be here soon," Laurie murmured.

He'd followed Alexis and Melissa to the couch, but instead of sitting with them, he was straightening the room. It was always a bit messy when Melissa spent time here, but Laurie had become great at cleaning everything. There were signs of his daughter everywhere, and every time Alexis noticed one, he couldn't help but smile.

"I'll go as soon as Melissa is done with her bottle," Alexis said. He hadn't yet met Candace, and he wasn't planning to anytime soon, even though he knew he should. After all, he was taking care of her daughter, and she was bound to want to meet him. She hadn't asked as far as he knew, and he wasn't going to offer. She wasn't just Melissa's mom. She was one of Laurie's exes, and Alexis had no idea what she thought of Laurie's mate taking care of Melissa.

Laurie stopped moving as he was about to pick up one of Melissa's blankets. He bit his lower lip, then grabbed the blanket and sat on the couch to fold it on his knees. "I was wondering if maybe you could stay?" he asked.

Alexis almost groaned. He'd just been thinking he wasn't ready to meet Candace, yet here Laurie was, asking him to.

He could say no, but he didn't want to disappoint Laurie, and he knew he had to meet Melissa's mom. "If you're sure? I don't want to push you into doing something you're not comfortable with."

Laurie nodded. "I'm sure. I've been thinking about it, and it's only fair that Candace meets you."

"Because I'm taking care of her daughter."

Laurie looked at Alexis as if he was an idiot. "And because you're my mate, and as such, you're going to be in Melissa's life for a long time, possibly all her life."

Right. There was that, too. "I wasn't sure you we're comfortable telling people were mates," Alexis said slowly.

Sometimes, it felt like no matter how many times they talked about being mates and what they wanted from that relationship, it didn't change anything. They were still awkward and barely touching each other. They might have all the time in the world to change that, but Alexis couldn't say he enjoyed the situation as it was now. He wanted more, no matter how many times he told himself he had to be careful.

"I am. My entire family knows about you, and they've been clamoring to meet you." Laurie frowned. "Except my mom. She's not really talking to me yet."

Alexis felt sorry for him. "She'll come around. She's still angry, but when she sees how good you are with Melissa, she'll realize that even though you didn't mean to become a father, you're a great one."

Laurie's cheeks flushed. "You really think that?"

"I do. You're great with Melissa, but even though you're still learning and sometimes you let stupid things get in your way, you've been working hard, and it shows."

"There's also something else. I need to tell Candace about me being a shifter, and I wanted you to be there when I do. I have no idea how she'll react, especially to the news that Melissa might be a shifter, too. I need support, and while I know it's a lot to ask, I can't think of a better person to ask it from. You don't have to stay if you're uncomfortable, though."

Alexis sighed. He should have expected this, but he hadn't. He'd barely even thought about the fact that Melissa might be a shifter or that Candace had no idea they existed. "I'll stay," he said. Hopefully, Candace would take the news well.

"What kind of shifter are you anyway?" he asked. He was pretty sure he already knew—the entire Long family was made up of swan shifters—but he wanted to hear it from Laurie.

"Black swan. What about you?"

"Nothing as exciting. I'm just a wolf shifter."

"Who told you it wasn't exciting? I love wolves."

That made Alexis smile. "That's good to know, since I'm your mate. You're kind of stuck with me."

Laurie wasn't, but Alexis had started pushing a bit every time he could to see where things stood between them. If Laurie freaked out and took a step back, Alexis would, too.

He didn't have to. Instead of moving away, Laurie smiled. "I'm looking forward to seeing you in your shifted form. Maybe we could do that for our date. It's been a while since I stretched my wings. I haven't had the time."

"That sounds like a good idea."

Laurie's eyes widened, and he bounced on the couch. "Why don't we go once Candace picks up Melissa? We could celebrate that way, or if Candace takes it badly, we'll need the distraction."

That wasn't what Alexis had in mind when he'd said he wanted to spend time with Laurie, but he didn't hate the idea. They wouldn't be able to talk if they were in their shifted form, but they'd find a way around it. Besides, they would be spending time in their human form before and after shifting.

"That sounds like a great idea," he agreed.

Laurie was still beaming when someone knocked on the door.

Laurie wished his life wasn't made up of secrets he had to disclose and people he had to shock. First, it had been his mother. Now, it was Candace, and he didn't know if he would be able to help her if she freaked out about him being a shifter.

Candace was human. Laurie had always known it, but he'd never told any of his girlfriends that he was a shifter. He hadn't needed to, not when they'd only been together a few weeks. Those women weren't part of his life anymore, and Candace hadn't meant to be, either.

But she was, and there was no way around telling her that he was a shifter, especially when Melissa was probably one, too.

Laurie's mother was a black swan shifter, while his father was human. Yet all of their seven sons turned out to be shifters, so the odds that Melissa would be one, too, were high. Laurie didn't hate the idea. He could already see himself talking Melissa through her first shift, then teaching her how to do it more easily. He could see them shift together and fly, play around, be a family. When he added Alexis to that image, things became even better.

None of that would happen if Candace didn't take the news well, though. It all hinged on her, and Laurie wasn't sure what he would do if she freaked out, grabbed Melissa, and ran away. His father had mentioned hiring a lawyer to put visitation rights and everything else on paper and sign all of it, but so far, Laurie hadn't had the time to do that. He hoped he wouldn't regret it.

He left Alexis and Melissa on the couch and went to open the door. Candace smiled when she saw him and pushed a blonde strand away from her face as she looked around

Laurie, no doubt searching for Melissa. Laurie moved so she could see her, and Candace's eyes widened when she saw her daughter's position.

She leaned closer to Laurie. "Who's that?"

Laurie rubbed the back of his neck. "My boyfriend." It felt strange to describe Alexis that way, but for now, he couldn't tell Candace that Alexis was his mate.

She arched a brow. "How come I never knew you also liked guys?"

"There's a lot you don't know about me," Laurie pointed out. His stomach churned, but he did his best to ignore it.

Candace walked in, and Laurie closed the door behind her. Alexis smiled up at her, but he didn't move to shake her hand since he was still holding Melissa.

"I'm Candace, Melissa's mother. Laurie told me you were his boyfriend?"

"I am. My name is Alexis. I've been helping Laurie with Melissa."

Candace frowned, then her eyes widened. "He mentioned something about a guy helping him that first day. Was that you?"

"It's how we met. He and Melissa were at the grocery store, and he was trying to choose diapers for her. I gave him tips and gave her her bottle."

Candace dropped her handbag into a chair and went toward the couch. "Well, thank you. I still feel horrible about dropping Melissa on him the way I did, and I feel better now that I know he wasn't completely alone in this. I was convinced he'd run to his mother, but I was wrong."

"You wouldn't have run to my mother, either, if you knew her," Laurie grumbled.

Candace looked at him. "I don't know. You make her sound like a dragon, but I can't wait to meet her and see if that's the truth."

Laurie had never really thought about that, but it made sense that Candace would meet his family. Even though she wasn't with Laurie anymore, they were both Melissa's parents, and Laurie had no intention of avoiding her or not having her in his life. Even if she found someone to be with, it wouldn't change the fact that she was Melissa's mother and he was her father, and he wanted them to get along and be a family. That included having Candace and Melissa over during family celebrations, or at least, he hoped so.

First, though, he had to do something. "Before you meet my mother, you need to know about her and the rest of my family," he started.

Candace frowned and sat next to Alexis on the couch. "That doesn't sound good. Are you a family of serial killers or something like that?"

Laurie spluttered. "We're not serial killers. God, do you hate me so much?"

"I don't, but you look like you expect me to yell at you, grab Melissa, and never come back. Maybe you should just come out with it, and we'll see what happens. So far, I'm expecting the worse, and I don't like it."

Laurie swallowed. There wasn't space for him on the couch, but he wouldn't have wanted to sit down anyway. Instead, he paced the tiny length of the living room in front of Candace and Alexis. "I know you read romance novels," he started.

Candace blinked but nodded. "When I have time, which right now, isn't a lot with the new job."

"What kind of romance do you read? Do any of them have werewolves and things like that?"

"You mean paranormal romance. Some do, yes. Where are you going with this, Laurie? Just spit it out. You're freaking me out."

Laurie stopped moving, standing in front of Candace.

"What would you say if you found out werewolves are real?"

Candace stared at him for a moment.

Laurie stared back, not knowing what to do. He'd never had to tell anyone he was a shifter. The only person outside his family who knew was Gilbert, and he did because he'd seen Laurie shift, not because Laurie had told him.

"What are you trying to tell me?" Candace asked slowly. "You're a werewolf?"

"Werewolves aren't real, or at least, I don't think so." Laurie looked at Alexis for confirmation, but Alexis just rolled his eyes and shook his head, and Laurie realized he was moving away from the topic of conversation. He cleared his throat. "Anyway, I don't know about werewolves, but shifters do exist."

"And you're one of them?"

"I am. And I'm not crazy, I promise. I can show you, if you want me to."

Candace rubbed her forehead. "This isn't what I thought you were going to tell me."

"It isn't how I thought you were going to take it." Because she was strangely calm, and she seemed to have accepted that Laurie was a shifter quickly.

"I already knew about shifters, Laurie. I just didn't know you were one."

This time, it was Laurie's turn to blink at her. "How do you know about shifters?"

"I'm friends with one. Her name is Celine, and she's a wolf shifter."

"That would be my sister," Alexis said. Melissa was done with her bottle, and now she was propped against Alexis's shoulder as he patted her back.

Candace's attention turned to him. "You're Celine's brother? She always talks about you."

"I am."

Laurie cleared his throat. "So, Candace, you know that Alexis is a wolf shifter. He's also my mate, by the way, not just my boyfriend."

Candace shook her head. "I'm going to have so many questions for you, but later. What kind of shifter are you?"

"A black swan."

Candace slowly nodded. "What about Melissa? Is she a shifter, too?"

Laurie didn't know how to answer that, and he was relieved when Alexis did instead. "She doesn't smell of shifter so far, but it's a possibility, and a strong one. She's young to shift, though. It will take time."

"Good. I wouldn't know what to do if she shifted and I found a tiny swan in her crib instead of her."

Laurie relaxed. This wasn't how he'd thought the conversation would go, but he couldn't say he was sorry it had. Candace wasn't running away screaming and telling him he would never see his daughter again. It didn't matter how many questions she had. Laurie would answer all of them if it kept Melissa in his life.

By the time Candace and Melissa left, Alexis was exhausted. He was still in his wolf form since he'd shifted to show both Candace and Melissa what he could turn into. He'd expected Candace to be wary, but she hadn't even blinked. She was obviously used to seeing Celine shift, and Alexis made a mental note to ask his sister about the woman when he next saw her.

Melissa, on the other hand, had found him fascinating. She'd pulled on his fur a few times before Laurie and Candace managed to get her hands away from Alexis, but Alexis didn't mind. He would rather have her learn how to be with animals with him than a real dog. At least he could be sure he wouldn't snap at her and hurt her.

Laurie closed the door and leaned against it. "That went so much better than I expected," he said.

Alexis looked around. It was time for him to shift back and go home, but he was pretty sure Laurie would be uncomfortable seeing him naked. He couldn't find the blanket he'd shifted under earlier, though, which was a problem.

Laurie pushed away from the door and came closer. He leaned down and retrieved a blanket from under the coffee table. "Is this what you were looking for?" he asked.

Alexis nodded. Laurie moved closer and settled the blanket over his furry body on the couch. Before moving away, though, he pushed his fingers into Alexis's fur, rubbing the top of Alexis's head. Alexis closed his eyes in pleasure. It had been too long since anyone had cuddled him in his wolf form, and he hoped that now that he'd met his mate, it would happen more often.

"You're impressive in this form," Laurie murmured. "Nothing like me. I'm just a big bird."

Alexis rolled his eyes at Laurie, causing him to laugh.

"I'm serious. I mean, swans are beautiful, but people usually hate them. They think swans are bitches, and I can't say they're wrong, at least not when it comes to real swans. But I'm just an oversized chicken. You're gorgeous, though."

Alexis shifted. Once he was back in his human form, he wrapped the blanket around his shoulders and leaned close enough to Laurie that he could swat the back of his head with one hand. "Stop that. If you're an oversized chicken, then I'm a dog."

Laurie cocked his head. "I suppose you are. So here we are, a chicken and a dog."

Alexis could see Laurie was teasing, and he liked it. They didn't usually spend time together without Melissa, and while he needed to go home, it was good to be here.

Still, Alexis couldn't stay forever, even though he wanted

to. "I should probably head out," he whispered.

Laurie stared at him. "Do you have to?"

"Well, Melissa isn't here anymore. You don't need me."

To Alexis's surprise, Laurie leaned closer. He pressed their lips together, then backed away, still staring.

Alexis was tempted to touch his lips, but instead, he asked, "What was that for?"

"Everything. You're such a good person that I can barely believe you're my mate. I don't want to stay away from you anymore. There's no changing what you are to me, or the fact that I'm falling in love with you."

Alexis swallowed. This was the last thing he'd expected to hear from Laurie tonight. "You are?" His voice was little more than a croak.

Laurie smiled deprecatingly. "It's kind of terrifying to admit it, but yes. I *am* falling in love with you. I don't want to stay away from you anymore."

"What about you not wanting to meet your mate?"

"It's still strange to think that you're my mate. I won't deny that or the fact that sometimes when I think about it, I freak out. But I can't imagine my life without you in it, and you've only been in it for a few weeks. I'm not stupid enough to think it would be easy to walk away from you, and honestly, I don't want to. I feel like you, Melissa, and I are a family, and I don't want to lose that. Even though this period of my life is the wildest I've ever lived through, it's also the best. I feel loved in a way only my family have loved me, which tells me a lot."

Alexis was afraid to ask his question, but he wanted to know. "What does it tell you?"

"That maybe we're a family, too."

Alexis beamed. When he'd imagined Laurie saying this to him, he'd thought they would be older, but he was happy that it hadn't taken Laurie that long. Some people might think they were too young, but Alexis didn't care. He and Laurie would work things out, along with Melissa, and it would be perfect.

Well, perfectly imperfect. Life always was, but as long as they had each other and Melissa, Alexis thought they could be happy.

"I'm still a bit lost, and I feel strange," Laurie continued. "I don't want to hurt you, even though I know that eventually I will. It's a strange feeling. I don't want to keep you a secret, but I'm also terrified to admit who you are to me, especially to myself. But I'm getting over it. I'm also dealing with the fact that I have no idea what to do when it comes to relationships. You're the first serious one I'll have and the last one. I already know I'll fuck up, and I hope you'll forgive me for that."

Alexis reached for Laurie's hand and took it. "No one is perfect, not even you."

Laurie snorted loudly. "I'm pretty sure I'm the most imperfect man in the world."

"But you're not. You've made mistakes, and you'll make more of them. We both will. But the important thing is that we're both willing to work through them and fix things. It would have been much easier for you to run away when Candace told you about Melissa and when you met me. You could have kept your life the way it was, but you didn't. You admitted you had to grow up, and you did exactly that. It won't be an easy or short process, but you've already started it, and that's all that matters."

"Are you sure it's enough for you?"

"For now. But I promise that if I have any kind of problem with you or what you're doing, I'll tell you. That's the only way we'll work things out between us. We have to talk, just like any couple, and maybe even more than them, considering everything else."

This time, when Laurie kissed Alexis, Alexis didn't let him

move away once he was done. He dragged him even closer, pulling until Laurie finally gave up resisting and climbed into Alexis's lap.

Alexis groaned when their groins came into contact. He'd been trying to hide the fact that he was hard, but now that he could feel Laurie was, too, he didn't want to anymore. Instead, he cupped Laurie's ass with both hands and pulled him even closer, pushing up so Laurie could feel what he was doing to him.

Laurie grinned. "Aren't we taking this a bit too fast?" he asked between two kisses.

Alexis suspected he was right, but he didn't want to wait anymore. They'd been cautious around each other, but he wanted to throw that caution to the wind and do what his heart—and his cock—wanted. "We can stop if you want," he said anyway. If Laurie was uncomfortable, Alexis was ready to do just about anything to change that.

Luckily for him, Laurie shook his head. "I don't want to. I'm just afraid to fuck things up. This is how I always do things when I meet people I like, but you're different. I don't want you to regret anything."

"I won't." Alexis kissed Laurie again to shut him up. He realized that no matter how many times he told Laurie he was fine with this, Laurie would still have doubts. He was terrified of doing something that would break them up, but he didn't realize yet that it would take a lot for that to happen. Alexis was in this for the long run, and so was Laurie. That was the only thing that mattered.

Well, that and getting Laurie naked. Alexis couldn't wait to see what Laurie looked like without clothes on, but to do that, he had to let go of him, and he wasn't happy. He growled when Laurie moved back, and for some reason, that made Laurie laugh.

He kissed Alexis's cheek, then scrambled to his feet. "Don't move. I want to look at you bare naked on my couch."

Alexis wasn't going anywhere. He pushed the blanket off his shoulders, exposing himself. Laurie smiled widely, and Alexis felt like the sexiest man in the world under his gaze. Still, Laurie didn't waste too much time staring at him. Once he had his fill, he pulled his t-shirt off, then quickly went to work on his jeans, huffing in frustration when he had trouble with the button. He solved that problem quickly, pushing his jeans down his legs, along with his boxers, apparently, since only seconds later, he was naked in front of Alexis.

Alexis looked, too. Just like he'd imagined, Laurie was gorgeous. It was obvious he took care of himself, because his body was trim and muscled. Not too much, but much more than Alexis's. Alexis wasn't jealous. The only thing he felt right now was the need to get his hands on his mate, so he opened his arms, and thankfully, Laurie came right away.

They didn't have anything to work with except their bodies, but maybe it was a good thing. Laurie was afraid they were going too fast, and keeping the sex simple might help with that. Alexis wanted more, but it could wait. It *would* wait, and he didn't even mind as Laurie settled back into his lap.

"Have you ever done this with a guy?" he murmured against the skin of Laurie's neck.

Laurie nodded. "I experimented in high school. I've never done this with my mate, though."

"Well, you're about to." Alexis gently bit down on Laurie's neck as he wrapped his hand around Laurie's cock. Laurie grunted and tried to push closer, the head of his cock dragging along Alexis's stomach.

Alexis kissed him again. He felt like he could never get enough of Laurie, and that was probably the case. Hopefully, he would feel this way for the rest of their lives, and for the first time, he couldn't wait to see what that would be like. Now, he had the certainty that Laurie would be in it, which helped a lot.

What helped even more was when Laurie wrapped his fingers around both their cocks. Alexis had to move his hand away, but he just placed it on top of Laurie's, since he wanted to be an active participant. They managed to cover their cocks with both their hands, and while it was nothing like being inside of Laurie would be, it was a nice substitution, at least for now.

They continued kissing as they pushed each other closer to orgasm. Alexis wanted to explore Laurie's body, and hopefully, he would have time to do that later tonight. For now, though, he focused on what they were doing in the moment, which was more than enough when Laurie looked like he was in heaven. His expression contorted with pleasure, and when Alexis felt his cock pulse against the palm of his hand, he knew his mate was about to come. That was a good thing, since he was, too.

He leaned down again and bit Laurie's neck for the second time. Laurie shuddered and cried out, semen splashing on both their stomachs. Alexis let go of Laurie's cock, wrapping his fingers only around his, then quickly jacking himself off. With Laurie still shuddering on top of him, his weight pinning Alexis on the couch, it only took him moments to add his own cum to what was already cooling on their skins.

Laurie flopped onto Alexis, and Alexis wrapped his arms around him. He felt Laurie's expression shift against his neck, and he smiled.

"You're getting my ass dirty with spunk," Laurie said.

Alexis hadn't meant to, but he rubbed his sticky palm around Laurie's skin, since he was there. "You have something against that?"

"Not as long as we can shower together."

"I've seen your shower, and I don't think we'll both fit in there."

"Spoilsport."

Alexis kissed the top of Laurie's head. "Next time, we're doing this in my place. My shower is big enough for the two of us."

"I like the fact that there'll be a *next time*."

"Me, too."

CHAPTER SIX

Laurie wasn't sure if today would be the worst day of his life or the best. Whichever way it went, it was bound to be a complicated one, and he prayed he'd be able to deal with it.

Because today, he was introducing both Alexis and Melissa to his family.

He already knew all his brothers would be there, except maybe Richie. As far as he knew, no one had been able to contact him, which worried him. He wasn't the only one to feel that way, but he wasn't sure there was anything he could do. He'd been an asshole and had never tried to contact Richie to ask him how he was, but he was aware of the fact that some of his brothers and his parents had. Richie hadn't told them anything about his life, and he sure wasn't going to tell Laurie, not when they weren't close. Maybe once this was over, Laurie could at least try to text him.

First, though, he had something to do.

He kept bouncing his knee in the car to the point that Alexis had to press a hand on top of it. "It's going to be okay," he said.

"You can't know that."

"Not for sure, but you also can't know it's going to be a disaster like you think it will be."

"What else could it be? My mother still isn't talking to me while my brothers always make fun of me when they see me, which doesn't bode well."

"Maybe your brothers made fun of you because they didn't see you as an adult. That's bound to change now."

Laurie snorted. "That's *never* going to change. I'm the baby of the family. They'll always see me that way."

Alexis frowned. "Being the youngest doesn't mean you're not an adult. You have a mate and a daughter now. Surely they can't deny that."

Laurie sighed. He didn't want Alexis to think his family was horrible. They weren't, not when Laurie thought about it and stopped obsessing over the teasing. Besides, they hadn't been the only ones who teased. He gave as good as he got, which probably didn't help.

"And Melissa is here," Alexis continued. "They're bound to be focused on her rather than on you."

"My father, maybe. Maybe even my mom."

"Melissa is adorable. I suspect your mother will want to talk to you, but you expect that, too."

Laurie did, and he hoped she would as much as he feared it.

He wasn't used to *not* talking to his mother for so long, but she was still angry, and he understood. Still, she'd invited him for Sunday lunch, and he hoped that he wouldn't disappoint her. She'd made a point of asking him to bring Alexis, but she hadn't mentioned Melissa. Laurie had no idea what that meant, but they were about to find out since he'd just turned the car onto their street.

He parked in front of the house and looked up at it. "We can still go back home. We could grab some fast food and spend the rest of the day on the couch."

Alexis smiled. "You don't really want that. I know you're anxious, but it'll be fine. Your family loves you. Never forget that."

Laurie sighed and got out of the car. Alexis wasn't wrong. His family, including his mother, loved him, and they wanted him to be happy. Hopefully, they would welcome Melissa with open arms. He wasn't sure what he would do if they didn't, but he couldn't just ignore this problem and hope it disappeared. It wasn't going to.

The door flew open before he even got Melissa out of her car seat. His brothers streamed out, and all headed toward him. Laurie took a deep breath, hauled Melissa out of her seat, and faced them.

"I half thought you'd lied," Andy said, stopping in front of Laurie and peering at Melissa. "But she's real."

Laurie rolled his eyes. "She is, and I'd like to take her inside."

When he turned around, though, Sean and Hugh were there, staring at Melissa, too. Laurie was pretty sure he could see a glint of jealousy in their eyes, and he grinned when he glanced at Leon and Peter, who were hovering on the porch as if they weren't part of the family. Peter looked slightly terrified, but from the look on Leon's face, Laurie was pretty sure he would soon lose Melissa to him and not see her until it was time to leave. He hadn't expected it, but maybe Leon and Hugh would be the next to add a member to the family — that was, unless one of their brothers found his mate, too.

Laurie ignored all of them and gestured at Alexis to follow him to the house. Once he stepped inside, he wasn't surprised to see his father waiting in the entrance. He beamed at the sight of Melissa, and when he reached out, Laurie was more than happy to put her into his arms. Once his hands were free, he grabbed Alexis's and pulled him closer. "Dad, this is Melissa, your granddaughter, while this is Alexis, my mate. Alexis, this is my father, Richard." Laurie turned around, saw that all of his brothers were inside except for Richie, who didn't seem to be here, and pointed at them as he introduced them. "Hugh, Andy, Jack, Sean, Curtis." He also introduced their mates, then added, "Everyone, this is Alexis. Leave him alone."

Jack snorted. "Fat chance of that. He's your mate, and you

remember what you used to say about mates. I want to know how he changed your mind."

Laurie sighed, but Alexis moved closer. "Don't worry about me," he murmured. "Focus on Melissa and your mother. I'll be fine."

Laurie wanted to believe him, but Alexis had never dealt with his brothers. "Are you sure?"

"I am. I promise I'll tell you if something is wrong, but I doubt I'll need to."

"They'll have a lot of questions about our relationship."

Alexis shrugged. "So? Our relationship is only our business, not theirs. I'm not going to tell them anything beyond what they're allowed to know. Don't worry too much. You have no reason to."

"Your mother is in the kitchen," Laurie's father said. He handed Melissa back to him. "You should go talk to her. She wants to meet Melissa."

"Are you sure?"

"Very much so. She hasn't been able to stop talking about her since she found out she had a granddaughter."

"Has she? Because she hasn't been talking to me."

Laurie's father sighed. "She's had a hard time coming to terms with the fact that you're a father. She'll come around, though. She loves you, and she'll never push you away any more than she already has. Talk to her. You'll see that."

Laurie swallowed and headed to the kitchen. He was relieved to leave his brothers behind, but he didn't think he'd ever been so nervous to talk to someone.

Just like his father had said, his mother was there, cooking. He saw her back stiffen when she heard him, but she didn't turn around to face him. Instead, she focused on the carrots she was cutting up. He swallowed again, then moved toward her. "Hi, Mom."

He expected her to ignore him, but thankfully, she didn't.

She still wasn't looking at him, but it didn't last long when Melissa gurgled and reached for her. She dropped the knife and turned around, her eyes wide.

"You didn't say you were bringing her," she said.

Everyone else had assumed he would, but not his mom. He wasn't sure what that meant. "I didn't know if Candace wanted to spend the day with her or if she would leave her with me. You can take her if you want. I think she wants to meet her grandma."

Laurie's mother rubbed her eyes. She wasn't crying, but Laurie was pretty sure she wasn't far from it. "You make me feel old calling me a grandma," she protested.

"You're not old. I realize that I shouldn't have had a child at nineteen. I know what you think about it, and you don't have to tell me again. But I promise you I was careful. I wasn't planning on this happening, but since it did, I'm dealing with it the best I can."

Laurie's mother finally took Melissa, who screeched and grabbed a strand of her hair. Thankfully, she didn't seem to mind, and she smiled down at Melissa as she pulled her hair out of her hold.

"I'm sorry for not calling you recently," Laurie's mom said.

Laurie shook his head. "You don't have to apologize. I'm the one who did everything wrong, and you were right to be angry at me."

"But not to ignore you. You're my son. That's never going to change. I have to accept Melissa, and I will. I have. It's good to know that you're aware of where you went wrong, though." She smiled at Laurie, and he felt like everything finally slid back into place. "I'm proud of you, Laurie. I've been doing a lot of thinking lately, and I realize I didn't tell you that enough. I and everyone else in this family have been viewing you like a child, but there's nothing further from the truth. You're not a child anymore. You're a father and a mate, and I know you'll do everything you can to make both Melissa and Alexis happy."

Laurie's heart felt like it was about to explode. "I already am."

Her smile widened. "Good. That's all I can ask from you, but I want you to remember that if you need anything, you just have to call me. I promise I won't ignore you ever again."

Laurie couldn't promise he would never fuck up in the future, but at least now, he knew he would always have his family.

Alexis was more nervous than he'd allowed Laurie to see and more than he'd expected. He hadn't wanted Laurie to worry, but it wasn't every day that he met his mate's family, and said family was so big. Alexis was used to having two siblings and his parents, and he could only imagine what growing up with six older brothers was like.

They were all nice, though. One of the brothers wasn't there, but all of the others were, along with their mates for three of them. They kept glancing at Alexis, and he was pretty sure that at least a few of the brothers wanted to tease him, but thankfully, they hadn't yet. Even if they had, it wouldn't have been a problem. From what Alexis had seen, it was goodhearted and similar to the relationship he had with his sister, although multiplied by five at the very least.

When Laurie came out of the kitchen, he was beaming. His mother was behind him, holding Melissa and looking delighted. Her smile widened when she saw Alexis, and she strode toward him. He expected her to shake his hand, but instead, she threw her free arm around him and hugged him to her chest. "It's such a pleasure to meet you," she said.

"Let him breathe," one of the brothers said. If Alexis remembered right, it was Andy.

Andy's mother ignored him, but she did lean back. "I know you're Alexis. Laurie told me about you. I'm Marie."

"It's a pleasure to meet you, too," Alexis said.

Melissa gurgled and reached for him, and he took her easily. It was only when she was in his arms that he realized that maybe Marie hadn't wanted to give her up. He looked at her to apologize, but her smile had shifted to something soft and gentle, and he was pretty sure she wouldn't ask for the baby. Alexis's cheeks felt hot, but he smiled again.

Marie shook herself. "I hope my other boys aren't giving you too many problems. If they are, feel free to tell them off or to come to me. They're all afraid of me, and I'll take care of them."

Someone made a strangled sound, then Jack said, "We're not afraid of you!"

His mother arched a brow at him, and he snapped his mouth shut. That made everyone laugh, including Alexis.

Laurie was more relaxed now that he'd talked to his mother, and Alexis could feel it when he sat next to him on the couch. Melissa was still in Alexis's arms, and she was babbling and looking around at all these new people. A few of the brothers looked wary, but at least one of the mates, Leon, was delighted. Alexis kept expecting him to snatch Melissa and run away with her, but thankfully, he limited himself to wiggling his fingers at her and allowing her to catch them every so often.

"She's adorable," he said.

Laurie puffed out his chest. "She's my daughter. She was bound to be."

Leon laughed. "I'm pretty sure you didn't make her on your own. Actually, you barely did any work."

Laurie's expression fell. "She's still my daughter."

"I never said she wasn't. She looks like you and your brothers, you know?"

Laurie squinted. "She does?"

Melissa really did look like him. Of course, babies changed as they grew up, so she might start looking more like her mother, but for now, Alexis could see Laurie in her brown eyes, in the shape of her nose, and even in her hair.

Alexis relaxed. Laurie had been afraid of facing his family, but he hadn't had a reason to. Even though his brothers were still teasing him, now that Alexis witnessed it, he could see they truly loved each other. There was no meanness in the teasing, and Laurie would have realized that if he'd allowed himself to. Instead, he'd gotten offended and had decided to go against his family. He'd done everything he could to show them he was an adult, but given the way they behaved with him, they already knew that.

Alexis was glad to be able to isolate himself for a bit when he had to change Melissa's diaper. He wasn't used to having so many people in the room at the same time, at least not in this kind of setting, and he was relieved to have a bit of silence. He'd insisted on being the one to change her diaper for that reason, and he sighed in relief once the door of the bedroom Marie had pointed out was closed behind him. Melissa wasn't happy, and she made it known, so he hurried toward the bed and dropped the diaper bag onto it.

"I'm going as fast as I can," he promised her.

He was halfway through when a knock on the door made him look up. "Come in," he called out.

He wasn't surprised when Marie came in. She closed the door behind herself, but she didn't come closer. Instead, she leaned against it and watched Alexis. He couldn't exactly stop what he was doing, so he continued and waited for Marie to tell him what was going on.

"I know I probably haven't made the best first impression," she said.

Alexis frowned. "I'm not sure what you're talking about.

You've been perfect today."

She waved his words away. "I mean when Laurie told me about Melissa. I didn't mean to push him away, but I needed time. It's not easy when your youngest son tells you he has a daughter. He's still my baby, even though I'm doing my best to treat him like an adult. It was hard for me to realize that he's not anymore."

"He might be a father, but he's still your son. He always will be. And you haven't made a bad impression. Anyone would have reacted the way you did."

"Maybe, maybe not. I'm having a hard time forgiving myself for that mistake, though. I'm glad Laurie has you. This isn't how I imagined his future would be, but it's not mine. It's Laurie's future and his life, and I won't try to push him in any way. It's hard to admit, but he knows what he's doing, and I can only be there for him when he needs me."

Alexis finished dressing Melissa and pulled her into his arms before turning to Marie. "I think he'll always need you. I imagined a lot of things when he told me about his family, but not what I actually found."

She smiled deprecatingly, and her smile was so similar to Laurie's that it was almost as if he was standing in front of Alexis. "You probably thought we were monsters. I know Laurie and the rest of his brothers have always had a conflicted relationship, although not in a bad way. But like me, they've always looked at him like the baby. They wanted to take care of him, but also to tease him. He never took that well, and I should have put a stop to it."

Alexis snorted. "How could you have? They're adults. It's not like you can forbid them from doing anything. Besides, there are so many of them. How are you supposed to keep an eye on all?"

Marie laughed. "I have experience in that, and it doesn't matter that they're adults. If I tell them not to do something, I expect them to follow the order."

Alexis laughed. "You remind me of my mother."

"I hope it's a good thing."

"It is. She's a bit like you. She's always had a strong hand, and she expects us to behave. Of course, she has it easier than you because she only has three kids."

"After the fourth, it didn't make a difference anymore."

Somehow, Alexis suspected that was a lie, but he didn't point it out.

He was relieved that Laurie's family was so accepting of him and Melissa. Even though he'd expected it from what he knew about them, he'd still been wary. It would be so easy to crush Laurie's hopes and his dreams, and he'd wondered if maybe one of Laurie's brothers would do that. Instead, even though there had been teasing, they were treating him like an adult, which was what Laurie needed.

After being seen as the baby of the family for so long, he was showing them that he wasn't, and they were accepting it.

Laurie was pretty sure he should go and rescue Alexis. He'd seen his mother slip into the hallway after she'd explained where Alexis could change the baby, and he suspected they were talking. He didn't know if that was something Alexis wanted, and he started to get to his feet to go and save him.

A hand on his arm stopped him.

He looked down at Sean, who shook his head. "Leave them be," Sean murmured.

Laurie settled back onto the couch again, but he was still worried. "What is she telling him?"

"Probably the same thing she's been telling all of us when she meets us," Leon said from Laurie's other side.

He seemed to be baby crazy, and he hadn't skipped a chance to be close to Melissa since they'd arrived.

"And what is that?" Laurie asked.

Leon shrugged. "That she's happy our mate has us. That we're welcome in the family."

Laurie looked toward the hallway. "Are you sure?"

"She's not going to eat him, if that's what you're worried about. I don't understand why you think so badly of your mother. She's a delightful woman."

Laurie huffed. "I never said she wasn't. Things aren't great between us, though. I don't want her to say anything that will spook Alexis."

"He doesn't look like the kind of guy who gets spooked easily, not even by mothers-in-law. I thought you and your mother had talked?"

"We did."

"Did you fix things, then?"

"I'm pretty sure she's still angry at me." And Laurie suspected it would take some time for her to get over that.

"Yes, well, it's not every day she finds out she's a grandmother. She'll get over it, though. It's obvious she loves you very much, just like she loves your brothers. Besides, she's been all over Melissa since you arrived," Leon said with a pout.

Laurie laughed. Leon wasn't wrong. Even though things were still slightly tense between Laurie and his mother, he could tell they'd fix themselves eventually. He just needed to give it time and show his mother that he truly was an adult and doing his best. "You wanted a turn at her?"

Leon's eyes glinted. "She's beautiful."

"I think you've already said that about a dozen times. Are you and Hugh thinking about adding to the family?"

Laurie had been watching his brother as he spoke, and he saw the moment in which Hugh paled. It made him feel kind of guilty, especially since Hugh was one of the brothers who had teased him the least. He'd always been kind of apart from the rest of them, and he was so much older that he and Laurie hadn't been close.

Leon sighed. "I don't know. We've never talked about it. Besides, we haven't been together that long."

"I don't think you need to have been together long to decide to have a child. Look at Alexis and me."

"You kind of did things the wrong way around. I wouldn't mind having a baby, I guess. It's not as easy as it was for you, which is one of the things that worry me."

Laurie didn't know Leon too well, but he could tell there was more on his mind. He didn't ask, even though he wanted to know. If Leon wished to talk, he knew where to find him. "I wouldn't worry too much. You and Hugh will be great fathers if and when you decide to have a child."

Leon's expression cleared. "You really think so?"

"I do. You're a good person, Leon. Don't underestimate yourself." Laurie didn't know what Leon had gone through in life, but he could recognize someone who thought they wouldn't be good enough. He'd felt the same way for most of his life, and he still did a lot of the time.

He *was* good enough, though. He was doing everything he could to be a good father to Melissa, and after Alexis had spent that night with him, they were closer than ever. Laurie knew that didn't mean everything was perfect, but it was as close to perfect as his life could be, especially so recently after meeting his mate and his daughter.

"So, what are your plans for the future?" Hugh asked.

He was probably relieved to move the topic to something else, and Laurie decided to humor him. "Well, I think I need to move. The apartment was good enough when I was on my own, but now that Melissa has been spending more time with me, I want a place that's safer for her, and possibly that has a bedroom for when she spends the night." She hadn't so far, but Laurie was ready.

Laurie looked up when Alexis, Melissa, and Laurie's mother returned to the room as he answered Hugh's question. Alexis smiled, and Laurie smiled back. He couldn't seem to stop himself.

There were a few *awws,* and someone made a retching sound, but Laurie ignored all of them and focused only on Alexis. Sean moved so Alexis could sit next to Laurie, and when he did, Laurie took one of Melissa's hands and squeezed it. She grinned a toothless smile at him, and something settled in his chest.

He looked around the room. This was where he belonged, even though for so long, he'd made sure he didn't. No matter how much teasing there was, the people around him were his family, and they cared about him. They wanted him to be happy and be successful in life, whatever that meant to him.

"Well, can't you find another apartment?" Jack asked. He kept his distance from Melissa, but Laurie hadn't missed the way he kept looking at her.

Laurie shook his head. "It's not that easy. The coffee shop job only pays so much, and if I want something bigger, I'll have to find a new job. I'm not good at anything, though."

"Don't talk about yourself that way," Laurie's mother protested.

Laurie was grateful, but he knew he was right. "There's not much I can do, Mom. Working at the coffee shop is easy, but it doesn't pay enough, and I'm not about to ask Roger for a raise." Even though Laurie was pretty sure he would give it to him, it wouldn't be fair. Roger would do it only because he knew Laurie's mother, and for once, Laurie wanted to do things the right way.

"Do you have anything in mind?" Sean asked.

Laurie shook his head. "I guess I want to do something that can give me a job for the long term. I don't want to go to college, but I'm not sure what I can do."

Sean hesitated. "Would you want to work with me?"

Laurie frowned. He'd never imagined himself working with his brothers, but especially not with Sean. Laurie had trouble seeing himself working construction. "I'd have no idea where to start."

"So? As long as you want to try and you do your best, that doesn't matter. You have to start somewhere, so why not there? I don't expect you to work for me for the rest of your life, but you could earn money and learn the trade."

"I don't know if I'll be any good at it."

"I doubt you will be, at least in the beginning. I promise that if there's a problem, I'll talk to you. Would that make you feel better?"

It would. Laurie's throat felt tight, and he didn't know how to thank Sean. "You don't have to do this just because I'm your brother," he murmured.

To Laurie's surprise, Sean grabbed and squeezed his shoulder. "I'm not doing it only because you're my brother. I gave Peter a job when he needed it, and the same goes for you. I want you to have a chance at whatever life you're planning, and that's not going to happen if you don't have a better job. I'm more than happy to give you one as long as you continue behaving the way you have lately. Act like an adult, be a good father to Melissa and a good mate to Alexis. That's all I expect from you."

Laurie was overwhelmed. He'd always seen his family as his nemesis, people who would never take him seriously. He'd been wrong, and he should have realized that sooner. "Thank you."

Sean squeezed again. "Don't worry about it and say yes. You can start as soon as you leave the coffee shop."

Alexis hadn't meant to start thinking about how his

apartment would be perfect for Laurie and Melissa to move into, but he hadn't been able to stop himself from doing just that.

He'd been looking for a roommate, and Laurie needed a new apartment. They were working things out between them, and Alexis truly felt like Melissa's stepfather now. He and Laurie were together, and even though things would never be perfect, they were as perfect as he wanted them to be.

His sister would probably tell him it was too soon for him and Laurie to move in together, and she might not be wrong. It could end up being a disaster, but it would make sense to do it. Laurie would move in with Alexis eventually anyway. Why have him move twice in such a short time and go through the trouble of finding a roommate that Alexis would have to ask to leave sooner or later when having Laurie move in with him right away would solve all those problems?

Alexis was dying to offer all of that to Laurie, but he wasn't sure it was a good idea. He certainly wasn't going to do it in front of Laurie's family, so he kept his mouth shut as they ate lunch, at least when it came to that.

It was easy to feel part of the family, and as time passed, Alexis relaxed even more. Once Melissa started fussing, though, he knew it was time for them to go home. Right now, home meant Laurie's apartment, and he was more than happy to drive Laurie's car while Laurie took care of Melissa in the back seat.

Once they were at the apartment, though, he couldn't stop himself anymore.

"You could move in with me," he blurted out after Laurie had come back from putting Melissa down for a nap in his bedroom.

Laurie froze and blinked at him. "I'm sorry?"

Alexis realized Laurie had no idea what he was talking about. He was messing this up, and he didn't want to. He rubbed the back of his neck. "You told your family you needed a new apartment, and I agree. This is a great bachelor pad, but you're not a bachelor anymore. Melissa needs her own bedroom, and I have a spare one."

Laurie slowly sat on the couch. "You mean the one that belonged to your roommate."

"He doesn't live with me anymore, and I need a new roommate. It would make sense for you to be that roommate."

"Would you want me to live in the spare bedroom, then? I could share with Melissa. It's not like she'll spend many nights with us for now."

Alexis rolled his eyes. He was pretty sure Laurie was teasing him, and while he didn't mind, his offer was serious. He sat next to Laurie and took one of his hands, linking their fingers together. "Think about it. You need a new apartment, and I need a roommate. I could find someone while you move, but how long do you think it will take us for us to decide we're ready to move in together?"

"I don't know. I don't want to go too fast, especially not when it comes to our relationship. It would be too easy for me to fuck it up, and I'd never forgive myself."

"You're not going to fuck it up. Hell, I have just as many possibilities as you to fuck things up. And if you truly don't want to move in with me, I'm sure I can help you find another place. I just thought I'd offer."

Laurie stared. "You truly mean that, don't you? You want me and Melissa to move in with you."

When Alexis focused only on what he wanted and not on the fear that something would happen and that they would break up, that was what he wished for. It was becoming harder and harder every time he had to leave this apartment and Laurie and Melissa behind. He'd been spending so much time here that he had several changes of clothes in Laurie's bedroom, as well as his toothbrush and his favorite shampoo and conditioner in the shower. He'd basically moved in, even though he and Laurie hadn't talked about it. What would change by moving all of their stuff to Alexis's apartment instead?

"I do," he confirmed. "I'm not a hundred percent sure, but that's only because I'm never a hundred percent sure of anything."

"Not even that you want to be a teacher?"

Alexis paused. "Except about that. But I realize that things aren't always going to be easy. I know we're going to fight, and we'll probably both regret being together eventually." Alexis swallowed. "But I don't think I'll ever regret loving you. You're my mate, and even though I have my doubts, there's no changing that. There's also no changing the fact that I love Melissa and that I want to be in her life. Besides, we've already been spending most of our time together here. I suspect that even if you move to a new apartment, that won't change. I want to spend time with the two of you, so why not just move into my place? It would make things easier for everyone."

Laurie was staring.

Alexis wanted to squirm, but since he had no idea what was going through Laurie's mind, he stayed still. He didn't want to push Laurie one way or another.

"You said you love me," Laurie finally said.

Alexis pressed his lips together. He hadn't meant to blurt that out, but he supposed that he wasn't surprised he had. "I'm falling in love with you, yes. It was always bound to happen."

"Because we're mates?"

Alexis dragged Laurie closer and kissed the top of his head. "Because you're one of the most infuriating and loving men I've ever met. Because I love seeing you first thing in the morning when you're still sleepy and your hair is all over the place. Because even though you have no idea what you're doing, you're working hard to be the best father you possibly can. Because even though it would have been much easier for you to tell Candace you didn't want anything to do with Melissa and sign away your parental rights, you didn't. You took the hardest path, and you never once looked back."

"Oh, that's not true. I keep wondering if I made the right choice and if maybe this is too hard for me. I don't want to fail, especially not at being your mate or being Melissa's father."

"You're not going to fail. It won't always be easy, but the thing that makes you a good father and a good mate is that you're powering through it. You want us to be happy, and you're doing everything you can to make that happen. That's another reason I'm falling in love with you." And Laurie was gorgeous, which didn't hurt. That wasn't what he needed to hear right now, though, so Alexis kept those words to himself.

Laurie sighed and wrapped his arms around Alexis's waist. "You have so much faith in me. I hope I won't disappoint you."

"You will eventually, just like I'll disappoint you. Our relationship isn't going to be perfect, but then, no relationship is. We just have to try. I promise that if you do something I dislike, I'll tell you. I expect you to do the same and for us to try to work things out together."

"My brothers seem perfectly happy with their mates."

And here Laurie was, comparing himself to his brothers once again. "I'm sure they are. Do you know the entire story, though? Are you aware of everything they've gone through before they landed on that perfectly happy life you mentioned?"

Laurie shook his head against Alexis's shoulder. "I haven't talked to them in too long. That's entirely my fault. I don't know what happened when Hugh and Leon met. Everyone knows about Curtis and Manuel, but not about Hugh, because Hugh is more reserved, but also because I've never tried to become closer to him or any of my brothers."

"And you can change that, too. Don't underestimate yourself, Laurie. You have the power to change your life and mine. You've already changed Melissa's, and you only had to accept her to make that happen."

Laurie tilted his head and smiled up at Alexis. "I'll move in with you."

It was all Alexis wanted to hear, and as he kissed Laurie, he could tell this would be the beginning of a good life. It was nothing like what he'd expected, but that wouldn't make it any less perfect.

CHAPTER SEVEN

L aurie had never expected to say this, but he was happy with his life how it was. He was only nineteen, yet here he was, with a daughter and a mate, and finally having made peace with his family, so much so that the family dinner his mother had demanded he and Alexis attended tonight didn't even feel like torture. For once, he wasn't running out the door as soon as the food was gone and had instead followed his father to the living room.

There were still some tensions between him and his brothers, especially Jack and Andy, who didn't seem to have gotten the memo that they needed to leave Laurie alone, but Laurie had learned to deal with them without pushing them away and isolating himself the way he had before. Besides, Laurie's mom was on his side. One well-placed glare from her, and Jack and Andy went back to walking the straight line.

All in all, Laurie had everything he'd never known he wanted.

He realized how lucky he was. Things could have gone so much worse if he hadn't met Alexis, and even more so if he hadn't decided to step up and be a father to Melissa. He knew that one of the reasons Alexis had given him a chance was because of that, and he was grateful every day that he'd finally managed to get his head out of his ass and become an adult. He should have done it a long time ago, but he supposed that it was better late than never.

Alexis leaned closer. "I have to say I'm glad Andy isn't here tonight," he murmured.

As much as Alexis had accepted Laurie's family, he still clashed with Andy and Jack, just like Laurie. Laurie didn't understand why they wouldn't leave him alone. He might be the youngest, but they were twenty-five and twenty-three years old. Weren't they supposed to be more mature than he was? Instead, they kept teasing him. As far as he knew, they still lived together and had nothing planned in life, pretty much like he hadn't until recently. They continued coming over to their parents' house for dinner and lunch almost every day, so much so that Laurie was surprised their mother hadn't kicked their asses out yet.

"He's on a date," he explained.

Alexis wrinkled his nose. "Who's so crazy that they'd want to go on a date with him?"

"Don't let him hear you say that. You know how he is."

Alexis arched a brow. "I can deal with him. I'm good at dealing with children who are throwing a tantrum."

Laurie barked out a laugh. "I wouldn't have described Andy that way, but you're not wrong."

"You're not the only one who has to do some growing up in the family."

"Shhh," Laurie said, peeking toward Jack. He might agree with Alexis, but he didn't want to fight. The evening was too nice for that to happen, and he was pretty sure that his mother would have something to say to Jack at the end of the evening anyway. Laurie wasn't the only one who was getting annoyed at the way Jack and Andy continued poking at him.

Alexis crossed his arms over his chest. "I have no problem telling them that their faces." He paused. "Do you want me to? Maybe they'll leave you alone then."

Laurie shook his head. "Just leave them be. The best way to win this argument is to be the bigger guy, and that's what I'm planning on doing. Besides, I have other things to focus on."

Alexis smiled. "You're enjoying the night off, aren't you?"

It was still strange to come over to his parents' house with Melissa and Alexis, but Laurie enjoyed it. He especially enjoyed watching his mother fawning over Melissa. As angry as she'd been when Laurie had told her about his daughter, she was the perfect grandmother, and Melissa adored her as much as she adored Melissa. Every time Laurie came over with the baby, she was snatched from his arms as soon as he walked through the door, and he only got her back when he was ready to leave. If it wasn't his mom, it was Leon or even Sean. He wasn't as rabid as Leon, but Laurie suspected he was going to have a baby conversation with Peter soon.

Melissa might be the family's first grandchild, but she certainly wouldn't be the last, and Laurie knew his mom couldn't wait to meet all her other grandchildren. Laurie wasn't going to give her another one anytime soon, but now that he had Alexis and he knew that dealing with a baby wasn't as horrible as he'd always thought, he could imagine them having another child sometime in the future.

A *long* time in the future.

For now, Laurie was happy, and he wanted that to continue.

A knock on the door made him frown. He looked at his father, who was sitting in his armchair. "Are you expecting anyone?"

His father shook his head and started to get to his feet, but Laurie raised a hand to stop him.

"I'll go." It was strange. The brothers knew not to knock because their mom didn't like them to, so Laurie doubted it was one of them. Andy, Hugh, and Sean, along with Leon and Peter, weren't there, and of course, Richie, but all of them knew to walk right in.

Laurie headed to the front door as whoever was there knocked again. He could feel Alexis right behind him, and it made him feel better. He flung the door open and froze.

"Richie?"

Richie tried to smile, but it looked painful. "Hey, baby brother."

Richie looked like he'd been beaten up, and Laurie suspected that was the case. His lower lip was busted, which would explain why smiling hurt. His left eye was swollen so much that Laurie wondered if he could see anything, and he could see a bruise blooming at the edge of his jaw. When Richie tried to step forward, he stumbled, and Laurie reacted on instinct, grabbing him. Richie hissed, but he leaned against Laurie, and Laurie helped him walk into the house. He was pretty sure there were more bruises he couldn't see on Richie's body.

"What happened to you?" he asked as he helped Richie lower himself into the chair in the entrance.

Alexis hovered by Laurie, clearly not sure what he could or should do.

Laurie crouched in front of his brother and looked up at him. Richie's hair was too long, which might be because he'd forgotten to cut it or on purpose to hide his eye. "Do I need to get you a doctor?"

Richie shook his head. "I'll be fine. It's not the first time this has happened."

Laurie hadn't realized he could be this angry. "Who did that to you?"

Richie grinned. "What will you do if I tell you? Will you go after him and hit him?"

Laurie huffed and leaned back. "No. I can't afford to do that, not with a daughter waiting for me at home. I can send Jack and Andy, though. I'm pretty sure they wouldn't mind doing it for me."

By now, the noise had attracted the rest of their family, and they were drifting into the entrance. Laurie's father swore and came closer, while Laurie's mother dumped Melissa into Manuel's arms and rushed to Richie. On the other hand, Richie couldn't seem to look away from Melissa, who was more than happy to be tugging on Manuel's hair.

"Who's that?" he asked.

"My daughter, Melissa. Are you going to tell us who did this to you?"

Richie shook his head and gently pushed away their mother's hands. "I promise I'm okay."

"You're not okay," their mom snapped. "That much is obvious, and you're going to tell us what happened."

"There's no need for that. I'm moving back home permanently, and that's all you have to know."

Laurie frowned. "When did you move away?" The last he'd known, Richie had been living in town.

Richie looked away. "I should have told you. I left town a few months ago, and it was the worst thing I could have done. That's over, though."

"Does it have to do with Francis?" Jack asked.

Everyone turned to look at him, including Richie, who looked like he wished Jack hadn't said anything.

"Who's Francis?" Manuel asked.

Jack looked more than ever like he wanted to pound someone into the floor. "Richie's boyfriend. Is he the one who hit you?"

It was more than hitting Richie. Whoever had hurt him had beaten him up, and probably more than once. Laurie hadn't thought he could feel this angry on behalf of one of his brothers, but right now, he wanted nothing more than to find this Francis and give him the same treatment he'd given Richie.

Richie tried to get to his feet, but their mother pushed him back into the chair. Unfortunately for him, his glare didn't look one bit threatening with the bruises and the swollen eye. "Don't stick your nose into this," he told Jack. "Whatever happened with Francis is over. He's never going to touch me again, and I want you to leave him alone."

So it *was* him. Laurie exchanged a glance with Alexis. He had no idea what to think of the situation or even what was going on, but he was sure of one thing.

They were a family, and they protected each other. If Francis tried to get to Richie again, he would have to face the wrath of Richie's six brothers — and several mates.

You may also enjoy the following from eXtasy Books Inc:

Black Savior
Catherine Lievens

Excerpt

Hogan had no idea what to do. He'd never had to help someone lay their egg, and he didn't know where to start. What if he did something wrong? Cain was writhing on the ground, holding his stomach and clearly in pain, and Hogan couldn't remember how to help him.

He knelt next to Cain. He was tempted to take his hand, but he didn't know how Cain would take it. "My name is Hogan," he said.

Cain breathed in and out, but it still took him a moment to look at Hogan. "Thanks for telling me. Are you male, female, or neither?"

"Male. What about you?"

"Same." He swallowed.

Hogan wanted to push Cain's hair away from his face. Cain was sweating, and the hair clung to his forehead. It was a pale color, maybe yellow, and Hogan wanted to touch it. Instead, he said, "I'll shift and let someone know what's going on."

Before he could get to his feet, Cain's hand shot out, and he grabbed one of his. "Please stay. I don't want to do this alone."

"I don't know how to help you." And it terrified Hogan. He'd never been one to want kids, even though he knew they were a blessing for the clan and the parents. He couldn't imagine himself with a child, and while Cain's wouldn't be his, he was pretty sure he would manage to fuck the kid up if he as much as touched the egg.

Cain shook his head. "It doesn't matter. It's almost over anyway. I just need you to hold my hand. Please."

He was begging, and it sounded wrong coming from his lips. Hogan more than ever wanted to shift and call for help, but instead, he knelt next to Cain, unhooked Cain's hand from his wrist, and linked their fingers together.

Cain was slightly taller than Hogan, but he was much slimmer, and his hand looked small in Hogan's. He was strong, though, and Hogan groaned when Cain squeezed his hand so hard he was pretty sure he would break it.

"Sorry, sorry, sorry," Cain chanted.

Hogan might never have helped anyone give birth, but he knew how it worked. He'd informed himself when Morven had gotten pregnant, just in case. Cain was working through the contractions, and from the looks and sound of it, they were coming closer and closer and were stronger than ever. He was right—he would be laying his egg soon.

Hogan swallowed. He could remember every word of the books he'd read about laying eggs and birth, and hopefully, it would be enough to help Cain. He had to keep his cool and focus. "You need to let me go," he said.

Cain shook his head. "I can't. I don't want to."

"I just want to check your pouch."

Cain's eyes snapped open. "Why?"

"To make sure everything is going well."

"You said you didn't know how to do this."

"Not practically, but I know the theory. It's better than nothing, right?"

Cain stared for a moment before nodding. "I suppose it is.

Fine. You can check my pouch."

Hogan wiggled his fingers once Cain let them go. Thankfully, nothing was broken, but they hurt a bit. He brushed it off and moved until he was kneeling between Cain's legs. His stomach was so distended that he looked like he was about to explode. That wouldn't be the case, but it still made Hogan uneasy.

He looked at Cain's pouch. It was opening, just like it was supposed to. It was also swollen, and the sight made Hogan shudder in horror. It was too easy to imagine himself in Cain's place, and he never wanted that to happen. No matter what his parents said, there was no way that going through this was a good thing. He didn't know why anyone would want to lay eggs, but he did know he never would.

He saw the moment the next contraction hit Cain. Cain threw his head back and his entire body tightened with pain. Hogan kept his gaze on the pouch, watching as it opened slightly more. He could see the egg peek through the opening, and he knew it was almost time. "Just a bit longer," he murmured. He wanted to soothe Cain, so he gently put his hand on Cain's thigh. He didn't know if it worked, but after a moment, Cain's body relaxed.

He was panting, and his body was damp with sweat. "How much longer?" he asked. He sounded exhausted.

"A contraction, maybe two. I promise you're almost done."

Cain nodded and flopped onto the ground. "This isn't how I thought it would go."

"You shouldn't be doing this on your own." Where was the egg's other parent? Cain was running from something, probably his clan, but that didn't explain why he was on his own.

"I'm not. I'm doing this with you."

Hogan opened his mouth to say something, although what, he didn't know. Before one word could pass his lips, Cain's body tensed again. He screamed, and the pouch opened wide enough that the egg moved forward. It wasn't quite enough for it to slip out, but Hogan knew what he needed to do. That was why he'd read those books, after all. He'd wanted to be prepared in case Morven needed him to do this, and he was glad he had.

He reached forward and gently slipped his fingers into the pouch. Cain's body convulsed under him, but Hogan kept his focus on the egg. He slowly slid it out, and Cain's body let go. It was more than ready for the egg to be laid.

Cain slumped on the cold earth, his panting the only sound in the forest. Hogan was holding the egg, and he was staring at it, fascinated. He'd never touched an egg or seen one up close. He hadn't expected to, either. He hadn't been about to ask Morven and Sheldon if he could touch theirs, no matter how much he wanted to. He might not wish to have children himself, but this was incredible.

The egg shone in the moonlight. It was a pale color, just like Cain, and slick with the fluids that have helped the laying. Hogan looked around for something to clean it, but before he could do anything, Cain sat up and took the egg. Hogan let go, and Cain cradled the egg against his chest, looking as if he hadn't slept in a week but also like he was ready to fight Hogan if he needed to. He would defend his baby, and Hogan's heart squeezed at the sight.

Cain shouldn't be this afraid. He shouldn't be doing this on his own or with Hogan, which was basically the same thing.

"I'll be going as soon as I can get to my feet," Cain promised.

The idea alarmed Hogan. "You can't."

"Why? Am I your prisoner?"

Hogan blinked. "Of course not. You've just laid your egg, though. You need rest and food, not to walk around the forest. Do you even know where you are?"

"In Ogorth clan territory. I'm just passing through."

Hogan arched a brow. "And where are you going?"

Cain hesitated, then shrugged. "I don't know. Wherever I can find a safe place to raise my baby."

"Not back to your clan?"

"Never. I'll run away if you contact them."

Whatever the Eiloren clan had done, it had been enough to send Cain running even though he'd known he was about to lay his egg. The thought made Hogan want to find all the clan members and tear them apart with his bare hands, but he had to focus on Cain first. He was an intruder, but Hogan suspected he had a good reason to be one. "I'll take you to the palace," he said.

Cain shook his head. "You can't. Your queen would have to give me back to my clan, and it's not possible. They would take my egg from me, and I would never see it again."

There was the urge to tear apart every single member of the Eiloren clan again. Instead of getting to his feet and flying in that direction, Hogan leaned closer to Cain. He was still kneeling between Cain's legs, and the position was an awkward one. He wanted Cain to trust him, even though he had no idea why. "The queen is a good ruler. She won't give you up if you don't want to go."

Cain's eyes were wide. It was almost as if he were trying very hard to keep them that way so he wouldn't fall asleep. Hogan had done it himself a few times, and he knew how hard it was.

"Why wouldn't she? I'd only bring trouble to your clan," Cain murmured.

"I know. If you need help, though, she'll give it to you. I promise." And if she didn't, Hogan was ready to fight for Cain and his egg.

He didn't know why. It didn't make sense, not when he didn't know Cain. Helping him lay his egg had brought them closer, and Hogan felt responsible. Cain's egg might not be Hogan's, but he'd helped bring it into the world. He'd been there when Cain needed him, and he felt responsible. He realized he couldn't make promises about what the queen would do, but he could promise his own behavior.

"Whatever happens, I'll make sure you're safe," he said.

"Even if it goes against your queen's orders?"

"Even then." Hogan was sure she would allow Cain to stay, but he was ready to shoulder this responsibility if she didn't. He'd promised, and he wasn't one to go back on his promises.

About the Author

Catherine is the creator of several series, most of them paranormal, including the Whitedell Pride Series and the Gillham Pack Series. While she graduated in translation, she decided to go the writer's way because it was more fun to create her own stories and characters.

She's been living in Italy for more than twenty years, but she's a daughter of the North—Belgium to be precise—and she misses it so much that she's already planning to move back.

She loves pizza—probably too much—her son, her pets, and of course, books. She sneaks some reading time into her schedule every time she has five minutes free from writing, demands from her various pets and son, and lastly, housework.

Connect with her:

lievens.catherine@gmail.com
BookBub: https://www.bookbub.com/authors/catherine-lievens
Website: https://authorcatherinelievens.com/
Facebook: https://www.facebook.com/catherine.lievens.9
Facebook Group: https://www.facebook.com/groups/411788002341528/
Twitter: https://twitter.com/authorCLievens
Newsletter: https://authorcatherinelievens.com/newsletter/